THE THREAD SHE UNRAVELED

Wives of the Vampire Queen 3

Sophia-Rose Johnson

S.R. Johnson L.L.C.

Published: S.R. Johnson L.L.C.
Editor: Susan Stradiotto, Bronzewood Books
Cover Design: Paige Eckman
Interior Design: S.R. Johnson L.L.C.

To my depressed girlies obsessed with vampires

WIVES OF THE VAMPIRE QUEEN SERIES

CONTENT NOTE

Before you begin reading, please be aware that parts of this dark fantasy book may be triggering for some readers.

The Thread She Unraveled depicts several difficult topics through either mentions or depictions: murder, blood drinking and blood play, sexual assault, consensual sex, misogyny and sexist behavior/ situations, death, violence, gore, suicidal ideation, menstruation, and more. While the whole book does not pertain to such topics, please remember to use self judgement before reading.

Take care of yourself.

I

Alone, Eudoxia walked beside the flowing canal. Snow piled on the stone edge, and flakes fluttered from the oppressing gray clouds, landing on her eyelashes.

Hidden in gray, she stopped for the smallest tick to watch herself in the water. The cool air of the oncoming winter stifled her lungs.

The longer she stared at her reflection, the more she thought she would fall in and drown. Worst of all, she would let that happen. They would have to fish her body out of the canal. Or maybe no one would notice she was gone, and her body would be lost under the oncoming thick winter ice. While people skated, her body would be pulled through the canals of the city and into the sea. She would never be found.

Children screeched, and something flashed behind her reflection. Just a swipe of gray as if a fast-moving bird but larger. Its features...human.

Startled, Eudoxia stepped back from the edge, fumbling with bundles of fabric, and faced whatever left her heart pounding. She thought she had seen someone behind her, but only children ran down the street, throwing snowballs at one another.

Eudoxia shook the dark thoughts from her head. No normal woman had thoughts like that...or they didn't speak them. At least, not to her.

For so long, Eudoxia had tried to be a normal woman, but she felt alien. Even when she left her old life and walked into the real world, she couldn't find a sense of belonging.

Gathering her skirts, Eudoxia—already late—quickened her pace.

When she entered the seamstress shop, the owner let her know it, snapping, "How far did you go? I only sent you down the street."

"They didn't have the order ready." The lie flowed from Eudoxia naturally, like pasting on a smile or ducking her head. "I had to wait."

Eudoxia placed bolt of cloth and thread on the table. The seamstress inspected the contents: her old, swollen knuckles brushed against the fabric, and her spindly fingertips grabbed the thread. Everything was as it should've been. Eudoxia had checked before leaving the merchant store.

Mistress Celine waved her away. "Get back to work."

The mistress fell into a seat beside the hearth, continuing her intricate stitching on a shawl requested by some passing merchant. Eudoxia never worked on something so lovely. Hopefully, someday. That type of dreaming would lead her to having her own shop, where she could create designs and choose fabric.

Eudoxia moved toward the back of the shop, but the mistress called, "Put the supplies away first!"

She gathered the cold fabric and thread, everything soft compared to the scratchy wool she worked on. Even the clothes on her back itched. She had to layer basically everything she owned just to be warm at night.

The mistress muttered under her breath, "Stupid girl. Send her back to the who—"

A bell dinged over the door, cutting off Mistress Celine's mumblings. She helped the customer as Eudoxia slipped the fabric and thread into their designated spots before walking into the back of the shop. The heavy curtains closed behind her, and she pulled her thick shawl tighter around her shoulders.

Several other women huddled together, their heads bent and fingers moving. They had a singular candle to work by.

"Took you long enough," grumbled one of the other women.

Eudoxia said nothing in return. She tried to ignore the sneer.

Taking her seat in the group, Eudoxia continued her earlier stitching. Her fingers were frozen, and she tried to warm them near the flickering candle.

The women whispered amongst themselves, asking about children and their lives, whatever gossip that they could scrounge up and share. Eudoxia had heard it a hundred times before. While the dukedom was large enough, the neighborhood drama was always the same.

Mistress Celine whipped back the curtain and glared, cutting off their voices. She no longer needed to threaten to dock pay or cut their work or terminate their employment. Her foul look was enough. When the curtains fell back into place, the whispers remained null. For the moment.

As the shop closed at dark, Eudoxia handed her pieces to Mistress Celine, whose downturned lips twitched. But she handed over the coins, which Eudoxia gobbled up. She didn't argue about the amount, even if the others did.

Stepping into the night, Eudoxia slipped most of the coins into her pocket for rent and then held the rest. As winter chill overtook her bones, she quickened her pace to keep warm, moving further inside the city. Her stomach rumbled. She wanted to drink until she barely remembered today.

Inside the pub, she rubbed her hands together for warmth, and one more fierce chill passed over her as she passed two women in a dark corner.

Eudoxia found an empty table in the shadows, paid for supper, drank one ale, and ordered another. It sloshed in her belly. She ignored how men ogled her, and when one began to saunter over, she turned her back on them. That left her facing the two women, who must've been less than half a dozen paces away.

The candles had been snuffed out around them. Two untouched mugs of ale sat on a round table before them.

"Come on, pretty lady." A man slid into the seat next to Eudoxia.

She stiffened but ate the food she paid good money for. She wasn't about to let it go to waste.

He leaned toward her, his breath smelling of old cabbage.

Trying to ignore him, she shoved a piece of old, dry meat into her mouth. Her teeth nearly cracked chewing it.

"I'm very persistent, and I know what women like," he said.

"I doubt it," said a woman.

Eudoxia whipped her head up from the meal that she had been so focused on.

One of the women who had been in the shadows now stood in front of Eudoxia. She had moved so quickly Eudoxia hadn't noticed. Eudoxia startled, clutching her ale mug.

The woman wore a long wool cloak and thick velvet dress with immaculate stitching, silver and gold woven into blooming roses on a deep purple. The work to dye that soft fabric must've been terrible. And the texture—all the harder to stitch in to.

Eudoxia balled her hand into a fist, resisting the urge to reach out and touch something so fine.

The man growled at the woman, "I wasn't talking to you."

"*She* is not talking to *you*," said the woman with a tightlipped smirk, the orange candlelight dancing off her dark eyes. "I wouldn't talk to you either. Look at yourself. You think you can lure a woman as the swine you are."

The man jumped to his feet, knees knocking the table. Eudoxia's ale sloshed in the mug, and she steadied it before she lost anything she'd paid for. Her stomach wasn't yet full, and she didn't know when her next good meal would be.

The pub had gone silent. Everyone had turned to watch the man and woman.

Obviously, the bigger and stronger man would win in a fight—but something about the woman....

Perhaps it was the amount of confidence she exuded. Not forced or arrogant, rather the way she held herself utterly still before the swine of a man, despite his flaring nostrils. The other woman from the shadows now rose from her seat, her plain but fine skirts falling to her leather boots. While she stood taller than the first, she didn't reach the man's height. She was as still as the woman closer to Eudoxia. As if she didn't breathe.

"What?" asked the closest woman, her voice a challenging purr.

This man puffed out his chest. "Do you know who you are talking to?"

"No," she dismissed, "but I bet it's no one."

She placed coins down on the table, like she was actually setting a bet, and then looked around the tavern and called out, "Can anyone tell me who this man is?"

Before anyone could answer, the man launched over the table. While drunk, he attacked quickly and had a massive wingspan. He reached for the woman, and he should've caught her. Instead, he landed on the floor where she had been standing. In the time it took Eudoxia to blink, and she had miraculously moved.

Impossible.

Off to the side, the woman flipped her hair over her shoulder. It bounced in curls.

The man scrambled to his feet as the second woman stepped forward. The shadows lingered in her dark hair, and she had her head ducked.

The drunkard swung toward the second woman, and she grabbed his wrist. He tried to jerk back, but she clung on.

Again, Eudoxia was sure she was seeing a miracle, but she didn't go to church.

The man crumbled to his knees while the woman towered

over him, holding his wrist. She never drew blood, but his fingers began to turn purple. Tears ran from the corners of his eyes.

"Don't like that, do you?" asked the first woman.

The second woman whipped her head around and murmured in a low tone.

Eudoxia thought she caught the name *Anna* but couldn't say for certain when the woman's thick accent touched the single word. Anything else she said was lost between them.

"Let go, bitch," the man whined, still trying to wrench back his arm.

"Or we could break your wrist?" said Anna, but the other woman released him that moment.

He slumped to his hands and knees, and the other woman commanded, "Go. Now."

He glared at them.

Eudoxia thought he might attack the women again. Everyone was waiting for it to happen, but he took whatever pride he had and stomped from the pub. Eudoxia thought it might've saved his life, not that she believed a fool like him wouldn't come back. They often did, their egos and cocks leading the charge into battle.

Eudoxia ate a bite of her now-cold chicken. It tasted like dirt, but it hadn't tasted good before. She needed to finish up her meal and go home, but first, she wanted to drink her ale in peace.

Anna sat in the chair opposite her and collected the coins from the bet. Eudoxia forced herself to swallow.

"Hello." She smiled, so gorgeous it hurt, and motioned to the woman hovering behind her like a bodyguard. "I'm Anna, and this is Xenia. And you are?"

"Not interested," said Eudoxia.

Unblinking, Anna raised her eyebrows. "You don't even know what I'm about to say."

"If you are not interested, then we shall go," said Xenia.

"Anna?"

Eudoxia responded to Anna, "I can guess what you want."

She had grown up in a whorehouse. These women had money, and they would spend it however they liked. They were dangerous, and it was dangerous to be around them.

The patrons around the pub eyed the two women. By morning, the rumors would hit the duke and the seamstress shop alike. Eudoxia should've left.

"I only want to see if you're well," Anna said demurely.

"I am," said Eudoxia.

Her last bites of food landed heavily in her souring stomach, but she wouldn't leave any behind. She knew better than to leave scraps. She regularly looked through compost bins for any leftovers.

"Come along, Anna," said Xenia, her voice distant. "Leave the girl alone."

"It's been so long since we had company." Anna spoke to Xenia over her shoulder, never taking her eyes off Eudoxia.

Xenia shook her head. "We need to eat."

Anna then broadened her smile, light flashing in her dark eyes. They could've eaten at the pub but hadn't. Women like them always had somewhere better to go—with heartier food and a warmer hearth and even fruity wine.

"Have a good life, Eudoxia," said Anna like she was talking to an old friend.

Eudoxia had never seen the woman before and was sure she would never see her again.

Arm-in-arm, the two odd women sauntered from the pub, cold air trailing in their wake. No one seemed to notice them leaving or how they left, almost like they were floating.

Eudoxia finished her ale in a few gulps, but before she left too, she wandered over to the dark corner. Two ales sat where the women had been, both filled to the brim. Eudoxia was still thirsty—a void in her not filled—and alcohol offered warmth in what would be her chilly apartment.

She downed the two mugs and wiped her mouth with the back of her hand, swallowing a belch. The ale was already wrapping around her, pooling in her feet and making her head swim. She needed to get back to her apartment. For once, she would fall asleep warm.

Stumbling from the pub, Eudoxia leaned against a wall. White breath escaped her mouth and clouded her face. She needed to keep some wits about her, so she tucked her chilling fingers into her cloak and hurried along.

Smoke burped into the sky, blocking out the stars like every other night, but it was worse tonight. Winter was always covered in constant clouds.

A whine echoed somewhere in the alleyway, and Eudoxia stifled her groan. She hoped she wasn't walking toward fucking.

She skidded to a halt in an alleyway smelling of blood and urine—both too familiar scents. She followed her nose like a hound, craning her neck.

A man was up against the wall as two women leaned against him, their hands traveling over his body. His head lolled to the side.

II

How much had Eudoxia had to drink? She was now imagining things... Maybe she was already asleep.

The man's feet didn't touch the ground. The two women had him pinned to the wall with their faces buried in his gut. He cried out, and one of the women slammed a hand over his face.

Eudoxia had no idea what she was seeing yet couldn't move. She was enthralled in how the women worked against the man, how they *ate* him.

While it was odd to think, she knew it was the right word. She couldn't remember the last time she had something juicier. No, *bloodier*.

Blood slipped down his body in tendrils, and his face grew pale like snow. His eyes were wide, a hand reaching toward Eudoxia.

Then she recognized him: the man from the pub.

One of the women followed his hand and looked back too.

Xenia—realization dawned on Eudoxia. And that had to be Anna with her.

How did they hold a man like that? Why were they killing him?

Why were they eating him?

Xenia dropped the man.

Anna complained, "What was that for?"

The man's blood rushed into the snow, and he slumped, his eyelids drooping.

"Look," ordered Xenia, inclining her head toward Eudoxia.

Anna stood in one fluid motion, her skirts fanning around her and a smile blooming on her face. "I told you, Xenia."

"What are you doing here?" demanded Xenia.

It took a moment for Eudoxia to realize the question was pointed at her. Even then, she stumbled over her answer.

"I'm going home." Eudoxia pointed at the man. "Is he dead?"

"He deserved it," said Anna at the same time Xenia ordered, "Go home."

Anna began to complain, but Xenia raised her hand to cut off the other woman and stalked toward Eudoxia. She barely made boot prints in the snow. No one would've known she was there when the dead man was found in the daylight.

Eudoxia had to tip back her head to see Xenia clearly. She was just as gorgeous as Anna, but her features were softer. It was her eyes that were stark. Determined. Hardened. The weight pressed into Eudoxia, making it impossible to breathe.

"You don't want to be here," said Xenia, her voice so calm it left Eudoxia blinking to keep her eyes open, "and you don't know what you saw. Go home."

Eudoxia was nodding before she knew it, but she would've done anything Xenia said.

Eudoxia had to pass by Anna to walk down the alleyway, and when she did, Anna leaned in and sniffed. Eudoxia quickened her pace as heat raged in her body. It pooled between her thighs.

Then she was back at her apartment, unsure how she managed to return, unable to remember.

Alcohol did that. It had been what she wanted when she began drinking tonight instead of saving her money for somewhere better than this. The apartment was a room she shared with other women, and she had a single trunk beneath her bed. Everyone else was already asleep, so she slid onto the hard mattress, rushing to fall asleep before the warmth wore off.

The warmth—thankfully—stayed with her all night, but it wasn't from the ale. Heat radiated in her lower belly and slipped from her thighs.

Morning came, and Eudoxia burrowed deep into her bed, warmth gone. Eudoxia was up before the sun and joined the fray to wash. When she changed dresses, she transferred her coin purse from one pocket to another. She had seen things go missing in this one-bedroom apartment with five women.

As Eudoxia walked the street, memories of last night flashed in her mind, but when she reached for one, everything was clouded like the sky. Her stale breath tasted of ale, but her skin smelled like blood. She didn't have monthlies because she rarely ate a full meal and illness threatened to take her every other week, yet the smell followed her. It was a surprise a stray dog hadn't caught her stench.

Her stomach grumbled as her nose caught a new scent. Something sweet. She paused outside a bakery. Those inside the frosted windows were maids and servants dressed in fine clothing, most likely collecting pastries and fancy breads for merchants and nobility. Mistress Celine's shop was near the wealthy part of the city, but Eudoxia stayed away from those houses and even servants.

The cold coins burned through the fabric of her clothes, but she put her head down and walked to the seamstress shop.

Mistress Celine, who lived in the apartment above, was already sipping tea and working. Eudoxia stepped in, gave a small head that hurt her neck, and went into the back. None of the other women had arrived.

Taking up her stitching, Eudoxia started mending. She never made anything different—Mistress Celine never allowed her—though she was sure she could if given the chance. However, those were dreams of girls who grew up with money. Those who had schooling and proper parentage. Not Eudoxia.

So she was stuck in last night's foggy memories, picking

through the shards as she worked. Her mind tried to piece them back together, only creating a hazy mosaic.

By candlelight, Eudoxia stared at the tiny stitches that she had sewn into the lining of a pair of trousers. She had taken the extra work when the woman with four children didn't arrive today. Of course, the other women then gossiped about her, clucking like hens.

The other women finished their work and began to seep away, but Eudoxia focused on how the stitches pulled the extra fabric. She wanted to rip out all previous stitches and start over, but the fabric would've torn.

A bell tolled in the front room, and Mistress Celine grumbled about her old joints. Womanly voices murmured, drawing Eudoxia's eyes away from her work. Her needle slipped.

Eudoxia gritted her teeth to stifle her groan at such a horrible stitch, trying to worm out the thread.

"Eudoxia, come here," called Mistress Celine in a singsong voice.

The unusual sweetness of the tone twisted her stomach.

The mistress called her again, some of the sugary sweetness gone, so Eudoxia went to the front of the shop. Her heels dug into the floor, planting her, as Anna—from the pub last night —studied one of the dresses the mistress created. It wasn't the mistress's best design, but she couldn't truly think of that when she stared at Anna. Eudoxia was sure she was a figment of her imagination.

"Come in," ordered Mistress Celine, her voice returning to the usual tone. "You're letting a draft through."

Eudoxia scurried forward, never ceasing her stare at Anna. Again, blurred memories of last night swirled; the taste of watered-down ale and hot blood curdled on her tongue.

Anna raised her eyebrows, like she was waiting for... recognition?

"Here she is," declared Mistress Celine. "Is there some sort of issue, my lady?"

"No," said Anna with a natural smile. She wore thick layers of dark clothing—the same heavy fabric from the pub—blending into the early night.

Eudoxia hadn't realized it had gotten so late, but it was better to be focused on stitches than the canal.

"May I question why you want to see one of my workers?" asked Mistress Celine. "This is my shop."

"So it is." Anna stepped toward Eudoxia. "I am looking to commission a new dress, and I was…led here. I believe you would be able to create something for the occasion."

"Why, of course, I can," said Mistress Celine.

"Your apprentice," corrected Anna. "Eudoxia."

The way Anna said her name sent a shiver down Eudoxia's spine.

She tried not to itch as the fabric of her dress became too thick. Too hot. It weighed on her shoulders until she felt like a melting pool of ice. Even then, a nagging voice in the back of Eudoxia's mind said Anna meant another seamstress.

Sugary venom lacing her words, Mistress Celine said, "She is not an apprentice. Just a stitching girl."

"Oh?" Anna raised her purse, and coins clanked around inside.

"She can be—is being taught. Still young, still learning," added Mistress Celine hastily, stepping closer to Anna and blocking Eudoxia from the conversation. "What is the occasion for the dress?"

"I am going to the duke's ball," said Anna.

At the mention of the occasion, a reminder of Anna's much higher station in society, Eudoxia finally looked away.

Anna would be going to the duke's ball with all the money she had spilling out of her purse. It was no wonder she was asking after Eudoxia; every other seamstress in the dukedom would be busy, creating dresses ordered months ago for the ball.

"His grace's ball?" The mistress's voice wavered.

Anna's eyes burrowed deep into Eudoxia, who was almost willing to give Anna whatever she liked.

Eudoxia rocked back to stop herself from sauntering across the floor and offering her body. She would've been no better than a girl in the whorehouse.

"I need a dress," said Anna, "and would like Eudoxia to make it."

III

Eudoxia tried not to gasp. Everything she had made was for herself and very plain, often patchwork to cover up a hole or reinforce the fabric. Never a dress for someone else. She had started working under Mistress Celine because she needed money and was good at sewing. The madam at the whorehouse said so.

"Yes, of course," said Mistress Celine. "Let us draw a few things up and pick out some fabrics. Return in a few days, my lady? We'll have something prepared to show you."

Eudoxia was unsure why the mistress said *we*. But she could barely hear anything over the blood pumping past her ears, much less speak. It felt like she was running through the alleyways, breathless, her vision darkening into pinpricks.

"A few days, then," agreed Anna.

"My lady," added the mistress, "we do need a down payment on the dress. Trying times and all."

Eudoxia could've laughed. In no way was the mistress having trying times, but Eudoxia thinned her lips together. No reason to anger the mistress now. Soon, she would see that Eudoxia hadn't fixed the trousers, which would send her into fury.

Anna withdrew a few coins from her purse, and the mistress bounced in a curtsy, her knees cracking. Anna backed away, giving one last pointed smile at Eudoxia, and then left.

15

Xenia stepped out of the shadows of the alleyway. The two of them walked on, arm in arm, like they had last night.

Before she knew it, Eudoxia had crossed the front room of the shop and looked out the window, her nose pressing to the glass. The two women had already disappeared, but Eudoxia didn't know how. Like last night, their footfalls hadn't left marks in the snow.

That wasn't the only thing impossible. Memories lingered just on the edge of her mind. Anna and Xenia, the man against the wall, the snow and the blood.

With a gasp, Eudoxia stumbled away from the window. Her heartbeat thundered. The room spun. She grabbed the edge of a nearby table to hold herself up right.

"I know it may feel difficult," said Mistress Celine, mistaking Eudoxia's gasp, "but don't worry. I'll whip up something for the lady."

Eudoxia put a hand against her chest, urging her heart to slow. "Anna said she wanted me to make her dress."

The mistress snorted. "The lady is confused. You don't make dresses. Never have—"

"I could," urged Eudoxia.

"You won't start now. This coin is mine, and this dress is mine. Do you know how long and how hard I've worked to get a dress into the duke's ball? This will be my start." She stepped behind the counter and slipped her coins into her purse. "Get back to work! I'm not paying you to dilly-dally. You have trousers to mend, and I have a dress to design."

She picked up charcoal and parchment, flipping through the designs.

In the next couple of days, Eudoxia did as Mistress Celine asked. The woman with four children was gone, and though many women asked about the open position, Mistress Celine was too busy to hire another because of Anna's dress. Thus, Eudoxia did Mistress Celine's work too. The other women, who complained about not having enough money, never took on more projects and never worked longer, and the mistress never paid them more. Then again, Eudoxia wasn't paid more either.

After all the women were gone, Eudoxia stabbed her needle through the fabric and pricked her finger. Blood welled up. She raised her finger to her mouth and sucked down her blood. The iron lingered on her tongue. The one bead rolled down her throat.

The candle was down to the wick, and the wax had melted into one clump. The flame flickered, about to go out, and it was time to eat and return to her apartment. She couldn't sew anymore today; her hands were no longer steady.

Setting aside her work, she swore she would finish it tomorrow and took what she had completed to Mistress Celine. With a huff, the mistress set aside her parchment and plucked Eudoxia's work from her hands.

Her nose was downturned, and she shook her head, clearly unimpressed. The same could be said for Eudoxia. She peeked at the mistress' work and found that its personality didn't match that of Anna's. Not the softness of her smile nor the cleverness in her eyes, like Anna knew the world's secrets yet never said.

"I don't think Anna will like this," said Eudoxia, tracing her finger along the broad brushstrokes. She had said it absentmindedly and wanted to reprimand herself for speaking out of turn.

"You don't know what she will like," muttered the mistress, pulling at Eudoxia's stitches. "Anna doesn't know what's fashionable, but I do. I know what all the high ladies are wearing, and I know what they should be wearing at the duke's ball."

"How?" asked Eudoxia. "We have no high ladies coming in here."

Mistress Celine slammed Eudoxia's work down on the table. "What would you know about that? High ladies and balls? You are a daughter of a whore. I gave you a chance, Eudoxia, and you're making me regret it."

"You regret it?" asked Eudoxia, voice pitching up an octave.

Anger washed over her. She had kept it locked away, but it burst as if the prick on her finger that drew blood would be her last.

Eudoxia scoffed. "I've been working myself to the bone to finish these items, and you haven't hired someone else. I'm doing your work too while you sit here and make designs that no one wants."

"How dare you speak to me like that!" Mistress Celine tried to jump to her feet, but she was an old woman and rocked back into her chair. "I don't need you and your insolence, strolling along the canal when you should be working. Leave now!"

Eudoxia's heart quaked, but fire burned through her veins.

She held out her quaking hand. "My pay."

"No."

"You cannot deny me my pay."

"I can," said the mistress. "I am your employer, and I find your work horrible. I will have to redo it."

"You've never had to before," said Eudoxia, panic dwindling through her veins like water in the canal.

Mistress Celine shrugged nonchalantly.

What would a woman like her know about going hungry or not having enough money when rent was due, rooming with other women? The mistress counted on Eudoxia and the others to do hard work because she did none of it.

Eudoxia lurched forward, reaching toward the mistress' purse. This money was hers! She needed it, damn it.

The mistress whipped a dagger from her skirt and slashed Eudoxia's hand. Pain seared her. Screaming, Eudoxia drew back, blood rushing from the wound.

Celine jabbed the dagger at her, so Eudoxia turned on her heel and ran. She left the door open, a trail of blood warming the snow. Celine would've never been able to catch her, but that didn't mean she wouldn't send the magistrate. It didn't matter that Eudoxia was only trying to take what was rightfully hers.

Meeting the canal, Eudoxia crumbled to her knees in the

snow and finally inspected her wound. Already, the bleeding was beginning to lessen, even if her palm still throbbed. The mark ran from thumb to pinky, and her fingers tingled. She tore the hem of her dress and wrapped her hand.

Blood dribbled on the snow, the crimson sizzling and melting into the dirt beneath.

Something else flooded her mind, and she closed her eyes, trying to follow where it brought her. It could only be a nightmare, because Anna and Xenia couldn't kill a man.

Water sloshed up the stone sides of the canal. Ice built on the edges, broken by the rush of waves coming via the tides. She hadn't heard of anyone yet this year stepping out on the ice, falling through, and drowning. She could be the first. However, no one would've believed it was an accident with how disjointed the ice was and didn't cross the canal in full.

Maybe she could just fall in. Already, her blood stained the ground. Others might think it was an accident, or she was attacked, but those ideas would be better than the fact that she threw herself in with no way to survive. No way to climb out and no one around to fish her out.

It would be simple to die like that.

Feeling as if someone watched her, Eudoxia squinted into the shadows. Buildings and houses waited along the canal, all of them dimmed for the night except for the occasional spark of orange from a hearth.

Picking herself off the snow, Eudoxia put her head down and walked toward the street. Others were out, tonight not as cold as the other nights. The wind had quieted.

With her money burning in her pocket and pride aching, she went into a pub and ordered an ale. And then another.

***

Someone pounded on Eudoxia's apartment door. Jerked awake from her deep sleep, she lifted her head. Nightmares had clawed in with blood, but they didn't haunt her waking. Drool dribbled from the corner of her mouth, and she wiped it away with the back of her hand. She met pain.

Gray morning light flooded her room, her roommates gone. She would've been gone too if she still had a job.

Another knock on the door, and Eudoxia flinched. Was the magistrate coming for her after what happened with Celine? No, because they would pounce on her. They wouldn't give her a chance to run.

"Eudoxia," called a man on the other side of the door.

She froze in bed, knowing that voice.

IV

Perhaps she could pretend she wasn't here. Or still asleep.

"I told the other ladies when they left," said the man, "but as a reminder, rent for the next month is due tomorrow. Eudoxia?"

Knowing she was unable to hide, she croaked, "Yes. I have it now."

She grabbed her purse from around her neck and pushed her hand inside, finding far less than expected. Certainly not enough to pay for rent. She whipped the purse off her body and tipped it over. Only a few coins fell out. She had more—where had they gone?

Jumping to her feet, last night's bad choices flooding her mind, she swayed. She now remembered where all her money had gone. She had drunk a lot at the pub. Her head pounded.

"Eudoxia?" asked her landlord from the other side of the door.

"I'll have the money for you tomorrow." She had no idea how she was going to get it.

Eudoxia didn't have a position and didn't know how to make so much in one night. She would be homeless by tomorrow tonight.

"Tomorrow morning," said her landlord.

No, she would be homeless by tomorrow at midday.

When her landlord was gone, Eudoxia hung her head. This was the perfect and most logical time to go throw herself in the canal, but it was the middle of the day. The last thing she needed was for someone to save her. She would have to survive in someone's debt and have no place to live.

After changing into her nicest clothes, washing herself, and rebandaging her wounded hand, Eudoxia sadly faced the day, hungover and hungry. She went to businesses that turned her away. They only gave one look at her to decide she wasn't worth the trouble, not with her drab clothes and mangled hand and the money she asked for so she could pay rent.

At one merchant, she mentioned she used to work under the mistress, not that Celine would give her a recommendation. The proprietor made Eudoxia show her needlework, but her hand hurt, and she couldn't hold a needle steady. She wouldn't hire herself.

Eudoxia stood at the edge of a dark street for a long time in front of a looming house. So many men walked into the whorehouse. When they came out, the men either walked like they owned the place or were huddled, hoods and hats pulled over their heads.

The latter men were spending whatever money they had on a fuck. They were also kinder and more appreciative than the men who threw money around and came here to beat the whores.

When there was a lull in the men entering, whores poked their heads from the windows and called to anyone on the street. They jiggled their tits, and it often gave men the last push to spend whatever they had. Eudoxia had seen men sell their souls to touch a whore's breasts.

One of the women poking out of the windows was the madam, looking like she hadn't aged in years. That was the last time Eudoxia had seen her. She wore such pale paint across her face, holding her skin in place. Her cheeks and lips were rouged in a mix of juice and arsenic. Charcoal was painted across her eyes.

The madam stared at her, but Eudoxia didn't move from the

curb. She could still walk away. However, her feet had brought her to her dead mother's whorehouse. She had been rooted in this spot for so long that she had seen several men enter and leave.

"Eudoxia, come inside already!" called the madam. Her voice was a high-pitched screech that made the other whores laugh.

Eudoxia rubbed the coins in her pocket. Her lackluster money. She had nowhere else to go, so she stepped off the side of the street and straight into the madam's waiting arms.

"It has been too long," said Corrine, brushing back Eudoxia's hair. "You look well."

"Don't lie," said Eudoxia.

She was skin and bones, nothing like the plush whores. They were well fed and had their own rooms. They were warm during the winter, and they had time to do leisure activities and money to spend. All they needed to do was give their bodies over to whoever paid.

"You look like shit," corrected the madam, leading Eudoxia inside the large house. "You're pale. Have you been eating?"

Moans and screams echoed somewhere down the hallway. Men fucked whores in common rooms. Only some went upstairs to the privacy of bedrooms. Men came in hungry, and they ate whatever was in their path, usually the first whore who smiled at them.

"Yes," said Eudoxia, just not as well as when she was a child here. "I lost my position yesterday, and rent is due tomorrow. I went around looking for a new job today, but I couldn't find one. My hand—"

"You need money, I understand," said Madam Corrine, tightening her grip on Eudoxia's shoulder. "Times are hard, and you are legacy. You've always belonged with us, Eudoxia."

"I only need funds now. I won't be continuing with this."

The madam raised an eyebrow. "I'll do this as a personal favor to your mother—may she rest in peace—and let you work tonight, but you know how this goes, Eudoxia. My girls are the best in the city, and we work on contracts. We have bills to pay."

Eudoxia had heard this all before. She had often given tours to the new women, showed them to their rooms, and stood close as the madam took them through the contract.

"I know," said Eudoxia. "Thank you."

Suddenly, Corrine pulled her into a nook of the house. "Are you sure I cannot convince you to stay? The men would like you. You're pretty."

Eudoxia pulled her shawl tighter around herself like it was a shield. She still felt exposed.

Corrine frowned. "See how it goes tonight, and we'll talk in the morning when you have your money. You will have to pay the house."

"I know." She had heard the contract since she was a child, cleaning pots and collecting the funds for the head madam, not Corrine at the time.

The madam jerked her head toward the staircase. "Let's get you changed into something nice. Though, I doubt any man would pass on you."

Even after she changed into a skimpy dress, brushed her hair, and painted her face with cosmetics, men passed by Eudoxia. It was like they knew she didn't want to be in the whorehouse.

Goose bumps had broken out across her skin with every gust of wind coming from the open door. She lined up with the other whores, and they were plucked from the line as night descended. Eudoxia remained. Even as the whores used once in the night returned to the line.

If she didn't get fucked, Eudoxia didn't get paid. Then she couldn't pay rent. She would be out on the street or might have to stay here like her mother.

Finally, her time came. A man in clean clothes in good repair sauntered toward her. He flashed his money. She went where he wanted, and he wanted it outside.

The winter chill hit her, and she shivered. He dragged her

into the small courtyard behind the house that in summer could be beautiful. There was no romance as he pushed her up against the cold brick, hiked up her dress, and plunged into her in one thrust.

The immediate pain morphed into discomfort. She tried to get into a better position, but the man pressed her face into the brick. The man thrust deeply into her. She groaned, and that only seemed to spur him on.

"Do you like it?" he asked.

He had a dagger strapped to his waist, and his boots were shiny. He had money but couldn't fuck his wife like this.

Eudoxia knew what she was supposed to say, so she said, "Yes."

She faked a moan that accidentally came out garbled.

The man gripped her hair and then slapped her ass. Pain sizzled on her skin. She didn't remember fucking hurting. He yanked back her head, nearly ripping her hair from her scalp. Stars bursting before her eyes, she let out a small scream, but he only fucked her harder.

"Tell me how much it hurts," he said, shoving so deep inside she felt like she was being stabbed.

Tears prickled her eyes, but she thinned her lips together, refusing to say anything. That was what he wanted. She couldn't allow herself to give in.

He grabbed her neck, and she tried to jerk away. That cost extra, and she didn't have to. Corrine hadn't allowed it before. He tightened his hand around her neck.

"Let go," she rasped, trying to claw off his hand, but he was so strong.

Her lungs burned for breath.

"Let go," she begged.

His fingernails dug into her skin as he tightened his hold on her.

She tried to scream—call out for help!

Wasn't there someone who had seen them go to the garden

together?

She could barely open her jaw. Every instinct was to continue to breathe.

Suddenly, he fell from her, and Eudoxia collapsed to her hands and knees.

Her mind was slow to restart, brain fuzzy from the lack of air, even though she knew she should've run. Instinct told her to, but she had crumpled, frozen to the winter ground, and she aimed her gaze to where he had been. Where his head now was, eyes staring into the distance.

His neck was jagged, skin ripped, and his blood pooled onto the trodden snow, seeping toward her. His body fell to the ground behind him.

Standing over his remains, licking blood from her lips, was Anna.

Eudoxia dropped back, fear rushing through her veins, and Anna's gaze snapped to her. Her dark pupils had narrowed to pinpricks. They grazed her neck. Her throat felt wrong, her skin tender. It would be easy to rip into.

"Oh dear, you're bleeding," said Anna.

In the blink of an eye, Anna bent in front of Eudoxia and wiped the blood off Eudoxia's chest and face. Eudoxia stilled as Anna brought that finger to her lips and licked the blood.

"You taste good," murmured Anna with a small girlish giggle.

While she was petite, the sound didn't match the power exuding from her body.

Her mouth dropped open, and Eudoxia mumbled, "Thank you."

It was what she would've said at the end of being fucked by the man, receiving her pay for her body.

Her pay!

She scrambled to the man and fished money from his pockets. He had only enough for a whore tonight. She expected more on a man who dressed so lofty, but it could've been an act. Many men played dress up for the whores, but the whores didn't care as long as they were paid.

Blood covered the coins, but she took the money for herself. It belonged to her after what she had endured.

"Does the body not bother you?" asked Anna.

Eudoxia had seen dead bodies before—claimed by illness, injury, childbirth—and memories of her mother's dead body flashed in her mind. She blinked them away.

"Corrine will pay someone to get rid of it," she said. "A man like him probably wasn't saying he was going to a whorehouse. If he's wealthy enough, people will look for him. They'll never look for him here."

"If you went missing, who would look for you?" asked Anna. The words were terribly soft, nearly lost in the breeze echoing through the garden.

Twisting around, Eudoxia peered up at Anna. "No one," she answered honestly. "I've been fired from my job, and this isn't enough money to pay for rent and I'm—"

"Going home with me." Anna offered her hand.

While the blood had been licked off, pink tinted her fingertips and palms. It should've terrified Eudoxia, especially as a few nights ago became clear. It wasn't a nightmare: she had seen Anna and Xenia in the alleyway, drinking a man's blood. He was dead too.

Eudoxia had faced death, but it hadn't grabbed her. Now, something new was being offered to her. Something that meant she wouldn't be a whore. In a life that had shown Eudoxia many hardships, they showed her kindness.

With her options limited, Eudoxia took Anna's icy hand, but Eudoxia barely felt it when she was already frozen. Anna wrapped her coat around Eudoxia, who had never felt anything so soft and warm. It was the softest kind of fur.

"Come along," said Anna in a kind voice, tugging her like a lost child in a crowd. "Let's get you something to eat and get you home."

Eudoxia went with her, not even stopping to collect

whatever she had in the whorehouse or back at her apartment. It was like she knew those things were of the past. She was entering a new future.

V

Last night was a nightmare...until it wasn't.

Much of yesterday had been enough for Eudoxia to throw herself into the canal, but when she reached where Anna and Xenia were staying, something changed.

"What is this?" demanded Xenia, hidden in shadows, yet her anger radiated like a blooming fire.

"You know who this is, my queen," said Anna, closing the door behind them.

Darkness consumed Xenia's penetrating gaze as it sent Eudoxia skittering back a step. Anna tightened her grip on her arm, holding her in place.

"What have you done, Anna?" demanded Xenia in a hushed, urging undertone.

Anna rolled her eyes. "I think it's clear: I have brought her here. She is to be our—"

"No," interrupted Xenia, turning away. "Speak to me in the sitting room. Away from Eudoxia."

Xenia stalked from the front entryway, leaving a gust of wind behind her. She melted into the shadows as if she hadn't been standing there at all.

"Maybe I should—" started Eudoxia, her throat aching.

Undoubtedly, she would have bruises in the morning.

"Stay here," said Anna in a soft tone. "I'll speak to Xenia.

Don't worry."

She brushed her thumb across Eudoxia's cheek as if brushing away a tear, but Eudoxia hadn't been crying. Had she? While her body was in pain, she felt numb.

"There should be food and wine in the kitchen. Just for you." Dropping her hand, Anna followed where Xenia had once been.

In the kitchen, Eudoxia tore into the food and drank the wine. She didn't question why the food was here—as if Anna knew she would come. She filled her pockets in case Xenia threw her out, knowing this might be the last time she could eat in days.

A little while later, Anna returned to the kitchen without Xenia. "Good. You've eaten. If you'll come with me, I have a bedroom made up for you."

Eudoxia gulped the bread that filled her mouth. "My room?"

"Yes. You'll be comfortable. And safe. I promise." Anna was quick to show Eudoxia to her bedroom and leave her, and Eudoxia was quick to fall into the soft bed, protected by a closed and locked door.

Eudoxia slept for a long time.

When she awoke at some point, gray sunlight slipping through the dark curtains, she lay in bed until her eyelids grew heavy. She fell asleep again. She awoke a few more times when it was light and then when it was dark. She heard someone outside her door as she curled into the soft bed and returned to sleep.

Unable to ignore her body's urges any longer, Eudoxia pushed out of bed the next day. While her hunger was stunted, her bladder could no longer take it, and she emptied herself into the chamber pot with a soft moan. She wiped sleep from her eyes and then looked back at the bed, considering. She was still tired.

It was when she spied her room that she truly awoke. The room was larger than the room she rented with five others. Dresses hung by the wardrobe, the doors open. She didn't think the dresses had been there before, but things were hazy from the night she had been brought to Anna's house. It had been so dark that she thought no one was home.

After dressing, Eudoxia opened the door to the rest of the house. She met silence. The hallways and the steps and the bedrooms were empty. She followed the cracking fire down to the kitchen. Food and wine waited for her, the only proof that someone else was here.

"Hello?" Eudoxia called, lifting a lit candle.

The drapes in the kitchen were pulled closed, and it was nearly impossible to see more than a pace in front of her. Eudoxia began to peel back a curtain.

A voice said, "Leave them shut."

She dropped the candle as she spun around. The flame went out. The hearth, the only light in the kitchen, illuminated half of Anna's face.

The shadows made Anna look a hundred years old, her ageless skin like porcelain. Her hair was out of place like she had just awoken.

"I—" Eudoxia swallowed. "Apologize."

She barely stopped herself from dropping into a curtsey, which was appropriate when facing a lady of Anna's rank.

"Don't be." Anna waved her hand dismissively. "I think you understand Xenia and I are...different."

"More than that," said Eudoxia. She tried not to cringe at how the words had flown from her mouth. "Where is Xenia?"

"Slumbering," she said.

Anna walked further into the kitchen, and Eudoxia stiffened. This woman was unlike anyone she had ever met. Then again, how many women did Eudoxia know who could rip a man's head off? Eudoxia tried to blink the blood-heavy memories away.

"Calm yourself," murmured Anna, holding her hands out to her sides. "I can hear your heartbeat. I won't harm you."

"I believe you," she said, but her heart didn't calm. "You

understand why I might be scared."

"I do." Anna sunk into a seat at the small table, nothing like the grand dining room that Eudoxia had walked through.

"You're very strong," said Eudoxia to fill the void of silence stretching between them.

"And fast," added Anna. "We drink blood."

Eudoxia gulped. "You drank my blood."

Anna smiled, albeit with her lips shut. "You taste wonderful."

"Do you plan on drinking my blood again?" asked Eudoxia, still rooted near the fallen candle.

She knew the flame offered no protection against women who drank blood. Terror sizzled in her veins, offering her the first sensation of life in a long time, but it quickly dissipated. How could she fear the women who saved her twice...even if they drank blood?

"Are you offering your blood?" asked Anna.

"No," said Eudoxia.

"Then no. Not at this time."

"You drink others' blood?"

"The life of a vampire," said Anna, like it was no small thing to drink blood.

"You and Xenia?" asked Eudoxia.

What Anna was saying was...impossible. Eudoxia could've still been asleep, or perhaps this was her afterlife. Either she had jumped into the canal or the man from the whorehouse had killed her. What kind of afterlife was this?

"Yes." Anna gave a small chuckle. "I really shouldn't be telling you any of this, but you've seen us drink blood and how strong we are. Xenia was not happy with me for bringing you home, but what was I supposed to do? He was going to kill you; I had to do something. Eudoxia, you are far too lovely to die."

She snorted. *Lovely?*

"What?" asked Anna, cocking her head to the side. "You

don't believe me?"

"No one has ever said that to me before." Her voice wavered as her mind wandered back to the canal. She didn't wish to think of it now.

"A shame." Anna worked her jaw. "The world is such a cruel place. Men are horrible, thinking the world belongs to them. Xenia and I have seen horrors. I couldn't let that happen to you, especially because you've seen bad things. I know it, Eudoxia. I can see it in your eyes."

She looked down at her hands. Her body was warm by the fire, and she hadn't moved away. Or any closer to Anna.

"Xenia will come around to you," continued Anna. "She must learn you. It's been a while since she has interacted with mortals. For, at least, extended amounts of time. I'm hoping you can change that."

"How so?" asked Eudoxia.

"We need help in the city," said Anna. "As you can probably tell, we're not from here."

"I have noticed," commented Eudoxia, but vampires couldn't need help from the likes of her. They were glamorous.

"What gave us away?" Anna smirked. "The blood drinking?"

Eudoxia giggled. She couldn't remember the last time she did that. She certainly wouldn't have laughed aloud at the whorehouse and have the men chase after her.

"Your accents," said Eudoxia.

Anna's laughter layered on hers. "Yes, we do have those. They're quite strong, aren't they?"

"Yes," she agreed.

"Like I said, we need help." Anna waved her hands like she was abandoning hope. "This city is closed off to outsiders, and we cannot go into sunlight."

Starting to understand, Eudoxia eyed the drapes. "Because you're a vampire?"

"Yes. We cannot meet others in daylight. We need someone to work on our behalf, keep up the house, and run errands as we navigate the city. In return, you will have a warm bed and a full belly and whatever you like. You'll have access to our funds. Oh, and you'll spend time with Xenia and me. We are enjoyable, promise. How does that sound?" Excitement rushed her words.

Eudoxia paused, having heard proclamations like this before. Usually, it was by men toward whores.

"Too good to be true," said Eudoxia flatly.

Anna frowned. "Because we're vampires?"

"Because I've been around enough people to know when a deal isn't as good as it seems," said Eudoxia. "What is required of me? My blood? If not mine, then whose? Shall I have to get rid of bodies like Corrine did?"

Smile faltering, Anna raised her chin in defiance. "We can handle our own. You wonder what will happen if you say no? What we will do? You'll be free to walk out the front door and never see us again. Take the dress with you too."

Eudoxia swallowed, eyeing the drapes and then the door.

There was nothing left outside for her. She had lost her bed and her things in the apartment, and she had no job or prospects. She would've had to return to the whorehouse and beg for a job, and Corrine might not offer her one—even as a favor to Eudoxia's mother—after the man had his head ripped off.

Eudoxia had two choices: the vampires in this house or the canal. For once, she didn't want the canal.

"All right," agreed Eudoxia, and Anna's smile broadened. "What shall I start with?"

VI

Working for Anna and Xenia was a combination of the seamstress shop and whorehouse, minus the fucking. It was more than she could've dreamed of, yet she was waiting for something bad to happen. Like Anna growing tired of her or Xenia telling her to leave.

While Eudoxia saw more of Anna than Xenia, when Eudoxia did see Xenia, the moments were short. Xenia gave a wide berth, and Eudoxia didn't move closer. Xenia seemed Anna's opposite: stoic and quiet. Anna wore bright colors to fit into high society, but Xenia dressed like a servant.

True to Anna's word, Anna and Xenia slept during the day, which left Eudoxia much time on her own. She had never been one for leisure activities—mostly because she didn't have the time or money—so what Eudoxia did on her own was drink, returning to the same pubs as before. She saw Anna and Xenia once out too, and while Anna had started toward her, Xenia gripped her elbow and towed her away. Eudoxia had tried not to take it personally. Employers did this.

Since Anna and Xenia weren't demanding of Eudoxia, she chose her own tasks in the house. She cleaned the many rooms they rented from a merchant away during the winter months. It was more work than one maid could do, but Anna and Xenia weren't messy. Until Eudoxia found blood.

It was only a small amount in the kitchen but made her halt. She could allow her memories to return, but the blood beginning to crust was a blaring reminder: They could kill her if they weren't satisfied with her.

Eudoxia, doing her duty, cleaned the blood off. The doorknob gleamed again, but the cloth was tainted pink.

Anna's stomach was strong enough not to churn at the sight of blood, but thoughts warped her mind of where the blood could've come from. Who had they killed to eat from?

Opening the door to the cellar, Eudoxia peered into the darkness. Blood was splattered on the ground. It slid down the steps and covered the walls. She slammed the door shut and backed away.

Anna never expressly told Eudoxia not to go down to the cellar, but Eudoxia also didn't need to be told.

Eudoxia had no reason to go to the high street but needed to be free from the house. She just had so many questions, though she never voiced them. The less she knew, the better. It was what she had done in every position she had.

Acting as a servant in proper attire allowed her into many places, and she used some of her earnings to buy herself a buttery pastry. It didn't taste as good as she thought it would. The sugary pastries had smelled nice, but her stomach was still jumbled after what she saw this morning.

"Did you hear about the dead body found last night?" gossiped one servant to another on the street, waiting to be let in a store.

Eudoxia leaned in. She didn't realize how much she missed speaking to others—or others speaking to her—until no one spoke to her much. She ran on a different schedule than the vampires.

"Another one?" asked the other servant. "What is that, three this week?"

"Apparently, their veins were torn open on their necks and wrists, torsos too," said the first servant.

The pastry soured. Eudoxia needed only one guess who had killed these people.

"Oh, don't look so sickly," said the first servant to the

second, both dressed in gray. "I know for certain that the latest man had two complaints filed against him for rape. He paid the magistrate both times."

"No one believes the girl anyway," said the second servant.

Eudoxia was aware. People hadn't batted an eyelash when Eudoxia had been harassed in the pub only for Anna and Xenia to save her, and no one had come when she was being choked by a paying man at the whorehouse. Except Anna.

As much as she wished to not hear the gossip any longer, Eudoxia was stuck in the herd of servants. If she stepped out of line, then she would be noticed for eavesdropping. The other servants either leaned into this new gossip—goodness knew the two servants talked loud enough—or talked amongst themselves about nothing good.

The first servant said, "People are saying it's a passing mercenary."

"Who is saying that?" asked the second servant.

"I am, but I'm not the only one. Can you imagine these men finally paying for their crimes?"

"What is done to them is going too far, don't you think?"

"No," said Eudoxia, pushing through the two servants and cutting away from the crowd.

Someone scoffed behind her, but she didn't slow. None of their feeble minds would ever understand.

Eudoxia stayed out for the rest of the day. She ate at a pub and then drank, stumbling back to the house with a too-clear mind from the cold winter air. She closed the servants' door and climbed up the stairs to the bedrooms, bypassing where the servants would normally be in a grand house. Nothing in this house was as it should be, including the moaning coming from one of the bedrooms.

It was a sound she was familiar with, but she never heard the moans of two women layered upon each other in such blissful harmony. This wasn't about fucking for money.

The sound wrapped around Eudoxia's legs, pulling her closer until she had her eye against the keyhole of a bedroom door.

Anna lay arched on a bed, Xenia hovering over her. They kissed. Their fingers traveled down each other's naked bodies. Anna kneaded Xenia's large breasts and pinched her nipples. In return, Xenia rubbed Anna's slit. Anna threw her head back as Xenia stroked her.

"Yes, my queen," said Anna, voice coming out as a whine. "Yes, Xenia. My queen."

The two of them fucked each other, their moans ecstatic. It choked Eudoxia.

The two vampires moved in tandem. Juices glistened their skin, tinged red.

Blood.

That was *almost* enough to make Eudoxia leave, but her hand cradled her cunt, having slipped up her skirts. She hadn't realized how she was massaging herself.

Eudoxia had heard many women screech and call men to be faster and harder, urging them like horses in a race, but these women took their time, exploring and loving each other.

A moan scratched against Eudoxia's throat, and Anna's eyes flickered to the door.

Had Anna heard? Or did she smell what was happening between Eudoxia's thighs? Her juices started to leak down her slit.

Anna continued to thrum herself against Xenia's body, but her eyes never left the door, even as she moaned louder.

Rocking back on her heels, Eudoxia stumbled down the hallway. Her heavy dress skirts twisted around her ankles like tentacles. She shoved through them. Slamming her bedroom door shut, she barely made it to her bed without ripping off her clothes.

Skimping to her underdress, she palmed her cunt. Her lower lips were puffy and sensitive, and she hissed when it felt so good. Leaning over the bed, she gained a good perch and fucked herself.

Pleasure moved through her, but she was already moaning as soon as she first reached her bedroom. She couldn't remember the last time she'd touched herself, the wanting overwhelming her.

As she rode her hand, she wanted more of this.

The pleasure.

The touch.

She wanted to be fucked by Anna. And Xenia.

Memories of their bodies and their moans spurred her hand to plunge further. She closed her eyes and imagined Anna touching her, Xenia sucking her, someone's fingers inside her.

Dots blinded her vision. Her breath caught in her throat, and her face heated. Fire spread across her skin.

"Fuck!" She gritted her teeth.

Blood rushed past her ears, and her heartbeat thundered. Was this what it was like to feel alive?

"Fuck," she repeated, shoving her face into the blankets.

When the orgasm dissipated, she slumped into the bed. Splaying her arms out, she reached for someone to hold her, but there was no one there.

VII

E udoxia waited for Anna.

　She considered entering the cellar, but as soon as she saw the blood still on the steps, she backed away. She had to wait until nighttime, and while darkness owned the winter, it took too long for it to come.

Eudoxia tried to keep busy, but all she could think about was her throbbing cunt. A lit fire in her wanted to gobble her whole.

When the sun finally set, Eudoxia ran to the kitchen, where Xenia was waiting with her head over a steaming pot, hair curling. A lump formed in Eudoxia's throat. Xenia turned to her and gave her an unnaturally looking tightlipped smile. The light failed to reach her eyes.

"I'm making you supper," said Xenia. "I hope you're hungry."

Eudoxia nodded. "I am. Thank you, mistress. Though, I should be making you supper."

"I don't think you mean that." Xenia flicked her eyes to Eudoxia's neck.

"Yes, of course." Her cheeks heated. "I mean, no. I don't. I won't be—"

Xenia held up her hand. "Please sit."

Reminded of her place in the house, Eudoxia sunk into a chair and looked at the dark cellar door. She squinted into the shadows, hoping to see Anna. The hearth crackled, yet the shadows were immense.

When Xenia turned from the stove, Eudoxia straightened in her seat. Xenia set the food on the table and then sat opposite Eudoxia in a fluid movement that made Eudoxia's hair flutter.

"Please eat," Xenia said kindly. Even in the few words, she embodied patience.

"What about yourself, mistress?" asked Eudoxia, eyeing the fish, bread, and squash. Should she trust a woman who drank blood to make something edible?

"You can call me by my name," said Xenia. "We may be employing you, but there is no difference between us. Mostly. As for my hunger, I have better control over myself than Anna."

Was it her name or the hunger that made Eudoxia's heartbeat quicken further? It thrummed under her skin. She fought the urge to touch the vein on her neck.

Xenia looked off the tip of her nose, and Eudoxia cut into her supper and ate a bite. It scorched her tongue. Still, she gave a small smile and a bob of her head in thanks. The food was surprisingly good for being made by someone who didn't eat, but Eudoxia didn't revel in the seasoned taste. She reminded herself to chew and swallow, repeating as the vampire mistress scrutinized her.

"Anna told me you watched us last night," said Xenia.

Eudoxia choked on her food at the sudden words.

Xenia was behind her in a flash, slapping a hand between Eudoxia's shoulder blades. The piece of food dislodged, but it felt like her rib cage shattered. With the food cleared from her throat, Eudoxia wheezed a breath, hands holding the table to keep her upright.

"I can also smell it on you." Leaning close to Eudoxia's neck, Xenia sniffed Eudoxia, nose in her hair. "Your arousal."

"I washed," said Eudoxia quickly, hiding her supposed crime.

She knew it had been wrong, but she wanted Anna. She couldn't have moved away.

"It lingers on you. And in your bedroom," added Xenia. "It wafts through the house."

Cheeks burning, Eudoxia stared at her plate. Her stomach was in such knots that she couldn't swallow another bite, let alone taste something without gagging.

Returning to the opposite seat, Xenia crossed her arms over her chest. While she wore a high-collared dress, the pressure on the fabric tightened it around her chest, exemplifying her large breasts. Eudoxia saw her in a whole new light, and she wanted to see what was hidden under the layers of fabric. She wanted to be close to those breasts, the nipples dark and long.

Eudoxia swallowed. Tears collected in her eyes, though she knew how foolish it was. How foolish she had been.

"I'm sorry to have seen you two last night," she said, trying to collect herself. Thankfully, she knew what she was supposed to say after years in a whorehouse and then as a seamstress. "It was a moment of intimacy, and I should've looked away. Will you be terminating my employment?"

"If I was to do so, then you would already be gone," explained Xenia. "Anna has a soft spot for you, like she does many mortals. I understand because I too have been mortal and seen vampires."

Eudoxia widened her eyes. "You have? Been mortal?"

"Yes. A hundred years ago or so," she said dismissively. "Not what you were expecting from vampires?"

Eudoxia blinked rapidly, trying to clear the new thoughts in her mind. Last night's memories swirled, warming her like the hearth did. She needed to focus on the Xenia in front of her, not who she had been even a mere night ago.

"I'm not sure what I expected. Probably more blood." Eudoxia regretted the words as soon as she said them, no matter how true they were.

"We are bloody creatures," said Xenia, still in an excruciatingly patient tone. "You have seen it when we drink blood, and we have been... *not as discreet* as we should be. It is why I think we should leave—"

"No!" Eudoxia clasped onto her hand, and Xenia stilled.

The chill burned her skin and then seeped into her bones. She didn't think she would ever be warm again, but she didn't release her hold.

"Please, don't. I beg you not to go," Eudoxia begged.

Tears welled in her eyes. The same anxiety and pain radiated in her body, though she didn't know where it came from or why it swelled now.

"Then it is Anna and I who need to become more discrete, but we have struggled here because we lack a blood source. We can drink from mortals without killing them, but as you have seen, we lack the ability to control mortals, specifically make them forget that they have seen us. It comes with age and practice, and we lack both," explained Xenia to Eudoxia like she was an old friend.

Eudoxia hung onto every word.

Xenia continued, "Having one's blood drunk can be pleasurable. Both Anna and I had our blood drunk when we were mortals and as vampires too. However, you must be willing, or it will be painful. Then death is probably preferable."

Eudoxia's mind slowly caught what Xenia was saying. "You want to drink my blood?"

She had known this was coming; she'd been waiting to be asked from the moment she learned Anna and Xenia were vampires. There were bodies in the city belonging to whoever they had drunk from, but never Eudoxia....

Xenia nodded once. "Anna said we wouldn't—it will be your choice—but you seemed *interested* last night. Drinking your blood would come with incentives for you as well."

"I already have what I need," said Eudoxia. A warm bed, her own room, food, funds.

"Then you are not interested, fine," agreed Xenia, withdrawing her hand.

Reaching forward, Eudoxia gripped the vampire harder. Her

fingernails broke against Xenia's skin. The shards bounced on the kitchen table.

"I didn't say that," said Eudoxia breathlessly.

If it meant Anna and Xenia's bodies upon her, then yes.

If it meant pleasure from them, then yes.

Anna sauntered from the cellar, wearing a form-fitting dress. Her grin took up the whole of her face. She must've heard what Eudoxia had said. Anna stopped behind Xenia and rested her hand on her shoulder. Xenia took her hand, holding her back from the moment. Anna leaned into her touch, tilting her head so her hair graced Xenia's fingers.

"Well?" prompted Xenia to Eudoxia. "Do you agree?"

Before joining their employment, Eudoxia often contemplated death. How she would do it. How there wouldn't be a mess. What death would be like and how no one would miss her. Those thoughts slunk away. Warmth grew in her heart, her mind, and her cunt.

"Yes," said Eudoxia. "I agree."

Her certainty wavered, but she forced herself to watch them.

"I'm so happy, Eudoxia! We'll take good care of you." Anna turned to Xenia. "Can I drink from her now?"

Eudoxia stilled. Were they doing this now? So quickly? She stared down at her food, wondering if she should've shoved it in her mouth or found an excuse.

"Slowly," advised Xenia in a warning tone. "We don't want to hurt her."

Released from Xenia's grip, Anna walked forward and took Eudoxia's wrist. Her fingertips were as icy as Xenia's, though it shouldn't have come as a surprise. Nevertheless, Eudoxia shuddered. They were truly doing this now. Anna trailed her fingers along Eudoxia's wrist and her vein and then knelt beside her.

"Relax, Eudoxia," said Anna. "It won't hurt if you're relaxed."

Eudoxia nodded, but it didn't calm her heart. Blood rushed past her ears as she anticipated the explosive orgasm she had last night. Was that what they meant by pleasure? She didn't understand how it could be so until Anna pressed her lips to Eudoxia's vein and licked it. Eudoxia jerked a little, the sensation like a tickle.

Anna arched an eyebrow.

Xenia waited behind her, a hand on her shoulder. It was like she meant to draw Anna back.

Lowering her head, Anna sucked on Eudoxia's skin. This was a new sensation, one that Eudoxia didn't know existed. It was so tender and promising.

Something nicked her wrist, and pain flashed across her skin. Anna's teeth were deep inside her. Eudoxia could feel how her blood was pulled to the surface with every suck. She latched her jaw, breathing heavily through her nostrils. Anna's tongue lapped against her wrist. Her lips traveled the length of her arm.

"Eudoxia, tell me how you're doing," commanded Xenia.

How was she?

What did she feel?

The pain morphed into pleasure.

"Don't stop," gasped Eudoxia.

Her eyelids fluttered shut, darkness overtaking her, before she forced her eyes open again. She watched Anna drink. She needed to see how the vampires worked.

Xenia lowered her head over Anna's shoulder and whispered something in her ear. Anna slowly detached herself from Eudoxia's arm. Eudoxia wanted her to come back.

"How are you feeling?" asked Xenia again as Anna licked her red lips, her skin glowing.

"Good." Eudoxia's single word slurred.

Pleasure wound through her, a different pleasure than what she experienced when she fucked herself. It felt good anyway.

"Do you think you can give more blood?" asked Anna.

Xenia shot her a warning look, giving a single shake of her head that was so quick Eudoxia nearly missed it.

"My queen needs to drink too," continued Anna.

"Drink." Eudoxia offered up her heavy, throbbing arm.

Winding her fingers around Eudoxia's forearm, Xenia set it back on the edge of the table. Her arm landed with a soft thud.

"Do tell me to stop if it is too much," said Xenia.

Eudoxia only nodded, searching for her tongue to string a sentence together. It would've been too much thought when she was floating.

Xenia sunk her teeth in, her fresh bite bringing pain. Eudoxia gasped, the pain receding. Anna had been soft but hurried when her tongue stroked Eudoxia's wrist, but Xenia was slow, gradual but precise with repeated beats.

More pleasure swept Eudoxia away. Her head swam. Her thighs brushed against each other sloppily, never getting enough purchase to grind.

Xenia pulled back and then slipped into the shadows of the kitchen. Eudoxia groaned. It was over too soon.

She wanted to reach for the two vampires and press their heads back into her body, but her limbs were weighty. She was sinking into the chair and then perhaps the floor. She would've melted through the cracks and seeped into the cellar.

"You'll feel better soon," cooed Anna before she looked up at Xenia, who stood next to Eudoxia.

Eudoxia startled. She hadn't realized Xenia was there but didn't know if that was her euphoric state that left her that slow or the blood loss. When had the vampire moved?

Xenia gripped Eudoxia's chin between her fingertips and opened her mouth, unlatching Eudoxia's jaw with ease. "I'm going to give you a small amount of blood, and it will heal your wound."

Eudoxia widened her eyes.

How much blood would turn her into one of them? No one had said anything about her drinking their blood, or was that when Eudoxia had been distracted by Anna? She always seemed distracted by Anna.

Xenia continued, "It won't taste very good but try to swallow."

In one swift move, she cut open her wrist and dribbled blood into Eudoxia's mouth with the same precision she had when drinking Eudoxia's blood. The iron coated Eudoxia's tongue. Trying to turn her head away, she gagged.

Xenia forced Eudoxia's mouth to remain open, and the blood ran down Eudoxia's throat until she felt like she was drowning in it. She swallowed one gulp, and Xenia let go of her chin. Eudoxia coughed.

The pain in her wrist and the buzzing in her head dimmed. She took deep breaths that faltered when Anna began to lick the blood from the table. Her long strokes ran the length of the wood. Xenia trailed her hands down Anna's back, and then they shared a blissful look. Eudoxia knew what they had coming and wanted to be part of it.

Anna turned toward Eudoxia, flaring her nostrils.

"Xenia," began Anna.

Xenia shook her head.

Anna whined, "She wants it."

"She doesn't know what she wants. She's controlled by the pleasure of our bite," said Xenia through gritted teeth. "You remember that feeling, don't you?"

"Yes," purred Anna, standing, but Xenia stood taller.

Their eyes were only on one another.

"I want more of it now," demanded Anna.

"Our guest first," said Xenia.

Unable to find words, Eudoxia nodded quickly, her head flopping like a dying fish. She wanted this—*them*.

Xenia folded Eudoxia in her arms like she was no more than a long feather, and Eudoxia rolled her head against Xenia's breasts. Heavenly. Soft. The kitchen and dark halls turned around her, and not even a moment had passed by the time Eudoxia was torn away from Xenia's breasts. She was deposited on her bed, and Xenia stood over her, Anna at her side.

"Perhaps we should change her," said Anna. "We don't want her sheets dirty."

"She is technically our maid," said Xenia pointedly. "She can do it. We should let her rest."

"I thought you never believed you stood any higher," said Anna as Xenia walked out of Eudoxia's bedroom, not participating in the blooming argument.

Anna bent beside Eudoxia, and Eudoxia tried to raise herself. She wanted Anna's lips. Eudoxia wanted her tongue inside Anna's mouth. And other places. She wanted to touch Anna's body, not just have Anna touch her. Then she wanted Xenia to return so she could pay homage to her wonderful breasts.

"Anna, come along," called Xenia from the hallway, her voice husky.

"Sleep well." Anna backed away.

They closed the door, and the house returned to silence.

Eudoxia didn't fuck herself last night, but she fell deep into dreams of bodies and moans regardless. When morning light came, Eudoxia had her fingers between her legs, wishing for more but only receiving an orgasm. Worst of all, it wasn't as good as it had once been.

After washing herself and stripping her bed, she set to her tasks. Last night's blood drinking had left no remnants; Eudoxia could've pretended it was an ale-induced dream. She rubbed her thumb over her bare wrist, not even puncture marks or tender skin.

Around midday, she went into the city and tried to avoid the hordes of servants. They were normally out in the morning, collecting everything before their employers awoke. Most servants in the afternoon trailed after their employers at a respectable pace but close enough to hear every drop of gossip. Eudoxia avoided those servants too until she almost stumbled into a herd that trailed after a woman surrounded by guards.

In the middle of the fanfare, the duchess wore a tiara that must've caused her to move at a snail's pace. Her hands trailed over whatever goods sat outside, and she eventually brought her nose to something a merchant offered.

Eudoxia hadn't seen the duchess since Eudoxia had been a child and traveled the poor streets handing out food and blankets. She had watched from the window of the whorehouse. The duchess never turned toward it, but her priests prayed outside.

The canal-riddled city was ruled by the duke and duchess, and they answered to a far-off king. Eudoxia didn't care much. For a child of a whore who barely had means, royalty was far above her. Nobility was best seen every few years.

Eudoxia turned away from the spectacle, gathering her cloak. She grabbed a few things from the market before returning to the house. Eudoxia made supper and ate—as Xenia had suggested she do—and Anna and Xenia joined her in the kitchen after sunset.

She offered her wrists and prepared for the pleasure she'd been anticipating.

VIII

"P erhaps we should take you somewhere more comfortable," said Anna. Her fingertips grazed Eudoxia's skin, tracing the vein.

Xenia traveled the kitchen, eyeing the food made and the half-empty plate. She gave a curt nod, like it was acceptable.

Eudoxia only said, "Whatever works for you."

She wanted them to bite her. To touch her. To hold her. She didn't allow herself to hope for more.

Anna lowered her head toward Eudoxia's wrist, but Xenia said, "What did you do today, Eudoxia?"

She gritted her teeth to hold back a groan as Anna pulled her head up, licking her lips. Eudoxia wanted to feed her. She would surrender her whole body.

Xenia rested her hand on Anna's shoulder. She wouldn't be allowed to eat until Xenia said so. It was almost vile.

"I went to the high street," said Eudoxia, searching her mundane memories. "The duchess was out."

"Did you speak to her?" asked Xenia.

"I'm only a servant," said Eudoxia, half amused and half astonished that Xenia would suggest it. The duchess would never talk to the likes of her.

"Oh, Xenia," said Anna, waving her hand. "You're too kind for this world. Of course, Eudoxia wouldn't."

Finally, someone understood.

"She should've," said Xenia, standing by the crackling hearth. She threw on another log, and the fire burped orange embers.

"Don't you have a ball coming up soon? That's why you came to the seamstress shop. You needed a dress." Eudoxia deflated, settling into her chair. The words bubbled up in her like she hadn't spoken in a very long time. "I didn't make you a dress—why didn't I make you a dress? You wanted me to make you one, and all the fashions in the city, and I—"

"It's all right," said Anna kindly.

"We have many dresses," said Xenia, scrunching her nose in confusion. "You want another, Anna?"

Anna flicked her gaze to Eudoxia, and Xenia rolled her eyes. It was another silent conversation passed between them; Eudoxia wanted to understand but feared she never would. She wanted to be between them and know their secrets as much as they knew each other.

Suddenly, Xenia's nostrils flared, and Anna smiled. It was cut off when Xenia shook her head, putting an end to whatever was between them.

"We are going to the duke's ball and already have dresses. Many of them." Anna clasped her hand tightly on Eudoxia's wrist, cutting off blood flow. "You should come with us."

"To the ball?" She wasn't sure she heard correctly. Or understood.

"Where else?" asked Anna. "Xenia, don't look at me that way. She'll be helpful, and she's been helpful so far. Eudoxia, you've been very helpful; Xenia is a worrier."

"We were dropping bodies in the city," said Xenia. "The magistrate was sniffing around."

"They don't suspect us. We've stopped now that we have Eudoxia to help us." Anna dragged her thumb over Eudoxia's thrumming vein.

Xenia grumbled, "It doesn't mean we should go to the ball."

In a flash, Anna was on her feet.

With a gust of wind washing across her face, Eudoxia startled. For living with vampires, she forgot how quick they were to move. Nor did she understand this blaze of anger now.

At her full height, Anna was still smaller than Xenia. Arms crossed over her chest, Xenia wore the same stoic face, one that was long when she looked at something hard. Anna was moving toward her.

Another silent message passed between them that could only be built up over a hundred years.

"Fine," relented Xenia.

Anna squealed before planting a kiss on Xenia's lips. Xenia slumped against Anna.

Whatever was happening between them, Eudoxia was the outsider and didn't know when her time would finally arrive to enter the world everyone else lived in.

Anna turned to Eudoxia, and Eudoxia puckered her lips like she would receive a kiss too. It didn't come.

Settling into the seat beside her, Anna said, "We'll get you a dress and go together."

"She'll have to be our servant at the ball," said Xenia. "Our invitation gave us no more guests, and we didn't mention originally that there were three of us."

"Then she'll be our personal handmaid," said Anna, words sharpened like daggers toward Xenia and returned to sugary sweetness when she spoke to Eudoxia: "It will be wonderful."

Eudoxia did believe it would be wonderful, especially as Anna sunk her teeth in.

IX

As Eudoxia stood before the mirror, she smoothed the soft satin of her ballgown. Her features were painted, so she looked more like a whore instead of a high lady. At least, that was how she felt. More layers of fabric covered her than when she ever lived in the whorehouse, but the makeup...

She wanted to scrape it off with her fingers.

Tear her skin away too.

Spill her guts all over the floor so the vampires could feast on them.

"You're gorgeous." Anna flounced over to Eudoxia and kissed her on the cheek.

While she was like ice, she left Eudoxia's skin warm and tingling. The sensation pooled between Eudoxia's thighs, her lower belly now heavy with need.

As a distraction, she looked at herself in the mirror, but the person in the mirror was the same as before: ugly. Unwanted. Lacking. A shell of waxy skin over protruding bones.

"You don't believe me, do you, Eudoxia? You're gorgeous. Just look at yourself." Anna touched her chin, forcing her to look at the mirror. As if Eudoxia didn't already see.

Eudoxia looked the same, but it was where Anna stood beside her that was empty. The mirror reflected the room like Anna didn't exist. Like this was all in Eudoxia's head.

"Xenia, come. Tell Eudoxia how gorgeous she is," called Anna.

Xenia glided into the bedroom as though carried by dove wings. "Stunning."

When Xenia stood beside Anna, the two of them were perfection in layers of skirts and jewelry, sparkling like fresh snow upon a calm canal. Each dress was cut for them; the jewels nestled between their breasts and collarbones and dripped from their ears. Eudoxia's heart almost exploded.

She hobbled away from them. Her dress was no longer pretty. She didn't want to see her reflection.

Anna began, "Xenia, we should—"

"No. The ball. Remember, Anna?" Xenia turned on her heel and strode from the room, skirts rustling and heels clacking. "The carriage has arrived."

Anna *harrumphed* and then held out her arm. Without hesitation, Eudoxia slipped her arm into the crook, and Anna locked her in place. She snuggled into Anna, though it was short lived. Anna slipped away from Eudoxia and next to Xenia, the two of them moving in quick tandem.

The carriage ride to the castle was surprisingly short—too short with how close Eudoxia was to Anna and Xenia opposite her. Their dresses layered each other, and their knees knocked together with every bump. Eudoxia's heart rattled her rib cage. She couldn't look at either of the vampires without feeling her core throb again. The sensation and the want had been growing until it threatened to consume her.

Anna flared her nostrils, and Xenia locked her hand around Anna before opening the window. Cold wind whipped into the carriage and carried out the floral perfume. Eudoxia again tried to suppress the growing sensitivity between her thighs.

When the carriage pulled to a stop outside the duke's castle, the two vampires stepped out, their dresses and jewels glittering. Eudoxia was a step behind them. She was, after all, only the personal handmaiden. She was slightly better than the servants.

The steps from the carriage to the castle had been cleared of snow, and up the steps, Xenia read off their names as *sisters*, no longer lovers. Eudoxia didn't have the chance to think it was odd because the butler asked with a sneer, "And her?"

"We need her close to us," said Anna hastily, and Xenia shot her a look.

Putting her head down, Eudoxia kept herself three steps back. She was aware how others watched her, some with hungry eyes. It was like she was back at the whorehouse, men wanting chunks of her. The servants, too, scrutinized her. She recognized none of them. Perhaps they felt she acted loftily when she was no better than them.

Anna and Xenia were escorted inside the castle brimming with people in fluffy dresses, fitted jackets, and so many jewels Eudoxia had to tamp her anger. It strummed through her, but she couldn't explain where it came from.

As Eudoxia peeked from her eyelashes, she knew who hired escorts for the night. The whores dressed and smelled nice, but the scent of fucking lingered. Too many memories swirled in her mind: all the times her mother had gone to balls and brought back stories and pieces of cake for Eudoxia, the nobility and rich merchants showering her with gifts that couldn't be worn or sold in case she was arrested for theft, the heavy perfume that masked cigar smoke. Eudoxia tried to blink the memories away. As well as her tears. She didn't want to ruin this night for the excited Anna.

An orchestra played in the ballroom as guests stood in line to meet the duke and duchess. Others hovered on the outskirts of the room, drinking and being merry. Eudoxia eyed the floor, acting as a handmaiden to rich merchants, but saw the puffy skirts and high necklines that Mistress Celine had wanted. Neither Anna nor Xenia wore such fashion, but it was more than their accents that made them different from the people in the ballroom.

"Your graces," said Xenia.

She and Anna swept into curtsies. Eudoxia dropped less than a tick later, her spine almost snapping in the corset.

The duke told them to rise, and Xenia was the first, then Anna, last Eudoxia. Whatever the duke and duchess said to Xenia—most likely polite talk—was lost to Eudoxia's ears from where she stood. She only heard the boisterous merchants and the strings of the orchestra.

With her head still bent, Eudoxia studied the duke and duchess. This was the closest she had ever stood to either of them. The duke was double the duchess' age, wheezing and trembling, but the duchess had crow's feet around her eyes now. Silver tinged her hair. She was as lovely as ever, but she looked old, almost ancient compared to Anna and Xenia.

The small conversation came to a close, and Xenia and Anna curtsied again, Eudoxia a second too late. They walked away. Eudoxia's knees trembled, and she was thankful for her new dress. It helped her pretend she belonged with Anna and Xenia.

Slipping through the crowd was surprisingly easy. Moving from their way, people stared at the two vampires, mouths ajar. It was very much how Eudoxia felt when she'd first seen Anna. When they moved, people craned their necks, peering around each other and pillars.

"I need a drink," mumbled Xenia.

Eudoxia immediately lifted her arm.

Xenia smacked her arm down and hissed, "I meant wine."

Eudoxia's cheeks heated, and she looked away. How could she be so foolish?

Anna laughed. "You'll have to excuse her, Eudoxia. Xenia gets odd about these things."

"I have my reasons," muttered Xenia.

Straightening, Xenia eyed the people around them. Others looked away, bowing their heads in shame. Eudoxia felt the need to do the same.

"I'm surprised you bowed to such lowly people, *my queen*," said Anna.

"Enough of that," said Xenia, and they smiled at each other.

Eudoxia cleared her throat. "Shall I get you wine, my lady?"

"Yes," said Xenia.

"Me too," added Anna.

"Of course, my lady." Eudoxia wouldn't have forgotten about her.

Anna was the sun on a cloudy day, peeking through to add brilliance to such a mundane life.

After a curtsy, which she only did because they were in public, Eudoxia shuffled to the filled wine goblets. She retrieved two goblets and returned to Xenia and Anna, who had been caught up in discussions with merchants and lesser nobility. They were newcomers to the city, and with money and the house they rented, everyone wanted to acquaint themselves.

So many men were in a line. Young and old, nobility and rich merchants, and whoever else paid to enter the ball tried to speak with Anna and Xenia, seemingly two unmarried sisters who looked nothing alike from a far-off land.

"Just one dance," pleaded Anna to Xenia, holding her hand.

"You're welcome to go." Xenia sipped her dark wine that she had been nursing for half the ball. "Have your pick. Or a few of the men around. You know they want it."

"Shall we take one home tonight, my queen?" whispered Anna.

Xenia shook her head and then added in a small voice, "Don't eat any of them."

Jealousy pooled in Eudoxia. She raised her head, not trying to show it.

"I'll try not to," said Anna.

She stepped away from Xenia, and the men descended on her like a pack of wolves. Now that she was a lone sheep, she was easy prey. Or so they must've thought. Anna sent a wink back at Xenia—and Eudoxia hoped herself—and chose a man to dance with. Her fingers grasped his wrist.

"Eudoxia," called Xenia.

She rushed forward the two steps and dropped into a curtsy.

Xenia waved her off. "I need you to stand next to me, so no men take it as an opportunity to speak to me."

Her voice had lost the patient note throughout the ball. Her body language also indicated she had lost her fortitude, looking like she would attack the next man that lumbered toward her.

"Yes, my lady," said Eudoxia.

Xenia smirked. "No one can hear us. No reason to call me that."

Eudoxia gulped. "I only do that because Anna calls you *her queen*."

Her smile broadened. "She says that for a different reason."

Eudoxia turned to the dance floor. Xenia wasn't looking at her anyway, and if Eudoxia looked at Xenia any longer, she might've started calling Xenia "my queen." She would praise Xenia like she was a queen.

While Xenia wore a thick dress with a mid-collar across her chest, the dress was cut in a way that exemplified her breasts. It had to be Anna's doing because Xenia rarely wore something like this. She even wore golden jewels with inset rubies, contrasting with Anna's silver and diamonds. The latter was plain for Anna, but she made up for it in her dress's dangerously—almost indecently—cut in the front.

Heat flamed in Eudoxia, and before she knew it, her thighs rubbed against one another. Her dress stuck to her moist skin. She swallowed the saliva buildup in her mouth. It only watered more when she looked at Anna on the dance floor. When she looked at Xenia, she almost came.

Xenia was looking back at her. She had to smell Eudoxia. *Had* to know everything.

Embarrassment most likely crossed Eudoxia's features, but she couldn't be mortified when she wanted them. She wanted their bodies pressed to hers.

Their tongues upon her body.

Their teeth deep in her.

Their fingers inside her cunt.

"Anna," called Xenia, her voice cutting through the chatter and orchestra.

The other vampire slipped away from the man she danced with mid-song. He tried to reach for her, but she swatted his hands away. The man grimaced.

She sauntered toward Eudoxia and Xenia, a coy smile curling her dainty pink lips. "Yes, Xenia?"

Then her body stiffened.

Eudoxia balled her fingers into her dress to hold her hands at her side, or she would've extended her arm again. She would offer more than her blood.

"We shall be leaving." Xenia strolled to the exit.

Eudoxia was about to follow, but Anna stepped in front of her. She took a deep whiff that left Eudoxia tingling from the brush of air. The small hairs on her arm lifted.

Anna moaned. "This'll be a fun night, Eudoxia."

X

Anticipation built so much in Eudoxia that her stomach hurt. With every bump on the road, she swallowed a moan. Her body had never reached this level of arousal before. Not even when she had touched herself the first time because of the vampires.

Watching Eudoxia under her thick eyelashes, Anna drank from Xenia's outstretched arm. Xenia was relaxed in her seat in the carriage, though she made no pretense of wearing a cloak to fight the chill. Her breasts practically spilled over the corset when she sat, and Eudoxia stopped herself from grabbing one of them.

She wanted Xenia's nipple in her mouth. To feel the temperature difference between Eudoxia's hot lips and Xenia's cold skin.

She wanted Xenia beneath her with her back arched as Eudoxia devoured those breasts. And Anna... What would it be like to have Anna's fingers stroking her slit while she gave endless bliss to Xenia?

There was so much Eudoxia wanted, but she was scared to voice it. She sealed her mouth, unsure what sound would squeak from her parted lips.

When the carriage rumbled to a stop outside the house, Eudoxia spilled out first, needing the fresh air to cool her heated thoughts. She stumbled when she slipped on the slick cobblestones, and Xenia caught her before she hit the ground. The vampire's iron-like hand hauled Eudoxia to her feet. Still, Eudoxia swayed as if she'd had too much to drink.

Xenia handed Eudoxia to Anna, and Eudoxia nearly fell into Anna's arms. Looping an arm around Eudoxia's shoulders, Anna took her inside, away from any prying eyes.

Once they were all locked away, the tense way the vampires moved vanished. They laughed and smiled, showing off their sparkling teeth, but they also moved naturally around their private space. Faster than they did in public, but also as though they were free to be themselves.

Eudoxia stared at Anna for a long time until Anna moved her toward the stairs, calling over her shoulder to Xenia, "Join us?"

"One at a time, my love," said Xenia, giving Eudoxia a flash of a smile. "We must lead Eudoxia into this slowly."

That might've been the first time Xenia smiled at her, and it melted Eudoxia's heart. But Anna had her attention now.

She grasped onto Eudoxia's waist, guiding her upstairs to one of the larger rooms with a massive bed. Anna led her over and sat her down on the edge. Eudoxia's breathing came in gusts as she imagined all the ways she craved both Anna and Xenia—spread across the quilt, naked and writhing.

In a flash, Anna vanished from Eudoxia's side to light the hearth, then she slowly undid her dress with a small smile playing at her lips. Eudoxia's heartbeat thundered so hard she thought it would explode. It almost did as Anna dropped her clothes.

The fabric pooled around her ankles, and Anna stepped out, revealing her perfectly lithe body. She sauntered over and stood before Eudoxia, then gripped the back of her neck, her touch cool.

Eudoxia wheezed.

"I'm going to kiss you now," said Anna.

"With your teeth?" Eudoxia asked, blinking up at the beautiful vampire with the most foreign of emotions—hope.

Whatever and however Anna wanted to kiss her would be fine. More than fine. It would be amazing. Life-changing.

Eudoxia licked her lips a split second before Anna's mouth came down over hers, slanting and driving her tongue into Eudoxia.

Anna had been soft and tender when she'd drank from Eudoxia the first time. Contrarily, this assault of a kiss was anything but gentle. Her lips were as hard as marble and equally as cold. Likewise, her tongue felt solid and frozen as though it were shaped from ice.

The rigidity of it left Eudoxia wanting to feel it moving between her legs. Her head swam as her heart pattered faster and faster in her chest. She lost herself in the sensation of a woman's kiss and embrace.

So different and refreshing.

Powerful, but gentle.

Unlike any man Eudoxia had ever kissed or fucked, Anna knew exactly what would please.

Whatever Anna did to her now was perfection.

Eudoxia, after all, was no breakable piece of glass. Her life hardened her to an extreme edge. As someone with nothing plush in her life, someone who often stared death in the eye, she needed to be hard to survive.

Until the vampires.

"Do you like this?" asked Anna.

Eudoxia loved it and nodded.

"Good." Another kiss and then Anna's cool tongue withdrew. "I'm going to undress you now."

Eudoxia gripped Anna, trying fruitlessly to force her to stay. Still, Eudoxia held on.

Anna laughed. "Do you not want to be naked?"

"I don't want you to stop kissing me." Eudoxia's lips buzzed, and she was hungry for another touch.

"That won't be a problem." Anna kissed her as she undid the

laces of Eudoxia's dress.

The fabric loosened, and Anna tugged it away. The weight fell off Eudoxia. From that moment forward, she would question wearing layers.

Anna trailed cool kisses down Eudoxia's now-exposed skin, and Eudoxia let out a yelp. Chills skittered across her body as Anna chuckled and then slid her tongue down to Eudoxia's stomach.

Eudoxia moaned and twisted her thighs together, hungry for friction.

Anna crouched and ripped away the fabric from Eudoxia's ankles. "I cannot wait to hear how loud you are when I fuck you."

Where there should've been a chill, Eudoxia only felt warmth, heated by the burning hearth and sparked by the lust in Anna's eyes.

"Lay back." Anna pushed her chest softly, and Eudoxia fell back on the bed as if she were tumbling into clouds.

Anna pushed Eudoxia's legs apart, and Eudoxia let her knees fall open, preparing for Anna's tongue. Instead, Anna placed her fingers softly on Eudoxia's slit and then sank into her cunt. Her thumb brushed the nub between Eudoxia's legs, and Eudoxia jumped.

She had only ever touched herself like this.

"Is this all right?" asked Anna.

"You said you wouldn't stop kissing me," said Eudoxia through rasping breaths.

"That I did." Leaning over, Anna joined her lips with Eudoxia's.

Eudoxia kissed her back, tasting her sweetness.

Sweat.

Blood.

Anna slipped her fingers out and back inside Eudoxia's cunt, and Eudoxia gasped, flouncing up. Anna pushed her down with her other hand, locking her to the bed, but never ceased her kissing.

Eudoxia's heels dug into the mattress. Her knees pointed toward the sky at either side of Anna, trembling with the effort to keep them parted. The pleasure mounted low in Eudoxia's belly, swelling and growing with each return of Anna's fingers. Eudoxia would never, ever get enough of this.

Anna swung a leg over Eudoxia's, and her drenched cunt met Eudoxia's thigh. Cooler still than Eudoxia's heated flesh, it drove Eudoxia to another height to know Anna craved pleasure from her as well.

Anna ground herself with primal force while tilting her hand to reach Eudoxia's inner pleasure point as well as her nub.

Unable to breathe, Eudoxia had to break the kiss. Anna trailed her lips down Eudoxia's neck and sucked, new layers of pleasure washing over Eudoxia.

Her hips rocked to meet Anna's thrusts, and Eudoxia's orgasm swept her up. She latched onto Anna, her lips falling open in a silent scream.

Moaning, Eudoxia wiggled on the bed as sensations rolled through her blood. A sense of soaring warmth flooded through her, and her thighs went tense, pulling upward.

Anna moaned when Eudoxia's leg hit her in the exact spot that she had been rubbing. The sounds she made heightened the ecstasy rolling through Eudoxia—a mixture of music and pleasure.

Eudoxia's core thrummed with a heartbeat of its own.

"Mmmm…" Anna hummed. "How was that?"

Anna wasn't even out of breath, and her hair spiraled down from the knot it once had been in.

"Wonderful," said Eudoxia. "Amazing. Impossible."

The words flowed out on her exhale.

Anna laughed. "Just you wait."

"For Xenia?" Eudoxia craned her neck to look around the room. "Where is she?"

"She went to get something to eat," said Anna.

Eudoxia huffed. She wanted to be the meal. She had been craving it as much as she had been craving their touch and an orgasm.

Giggling, Anna patted Eudoxia's thigh. "Don't worry. She's much better at not dropping a body. No one will know."

"She could've drunk from me," said Eudoxia.

"She still might, but she's cautious. She has had to be." She dragged her fingers the length of Eudoxia's arm. "I still might too. You've made me hungry."

Yes, she wanted to feed Anna. Also Xenia, who was more than cautious. She was patiently cold, hovering in the shadows.

"Is she cautious because she's a vampire?" asked Eudoxia.

"Because she's a queen," said Anna, raising her eyebrows. "You didn't know that, did you? Well, she is, not that she'll take the title or announce it to the world or wear the crowns that she should. I pray to her in every way that I can, much of it is in sex. I'll pray to her in—"

"What way exactly?" Xenia stood in the doorway, her body exposed.

XI

Xenia crossed her arms over her chest, her breasts bubbling up. The rest of her was plump and pale, and Eudoxia wanted to reach out and touch her *everywhere*. There was so much to discover on Xenia's body.

"However you like, my queen." Anna patted the bed beside Eudoxia. "Won't you join us?"

Xenia walked to the edge of the mattress but then brushed past, and Anna frowned. She settled in a chair and draped one leg over the arm, exposing her cunt.

Eudoxia's mouth watered.

"How was supper?" asked Anna, licking her lips.

"Delicious." Xenia grabbed her breast and then put her other hand to her cunt, starting to massage slowly.

She parted her lower lips, revealing the path inside. Xenia rubbed her clit like it was an afterthought.

Eudoxia had never fucked herself so slowly. When she needed to come, it had been rushed.

Xenia rolled her hips as her hand danced across her cunt. She tipped up her massive breast and took her nipple in her mouth, nibbling.

Eudoxia bit her bottom lip as if she could pretend it was Xenia's nipple. To feel the soft skin between her teeth, the grooves on her areola as she licked.

Xenia slipped her fingers deep, stretching herself wide. Eudoxia's gaze clung to every movement. She could crawl inside her and fuck her hollow, wringing from the vampire a climax that would break into screams, her name echoing like thunderous applause.

Anna moved in a flash, leaving nothing but a breeze to chill Eudoxia. In the blink of an eye, she knelt between Xenia's legs and buried her face.

Eudoxia wanted to do that but lacked the speed. Still, she rolled to her trembling knees to get closer.

Anna drank Xenia's juices, slurping so much they ran from her chin like she'd taken a bite from ripe fruit. Eudoxia sniffed them in the air, wanting more, but she was stranded on the bed, so she slipped her hands between her own thighs. She listened to how Xenia moaned and touched herself where Anna's fingers had been.

Where she wanted Anna's fingers to be in again.

Anna's juices had leaked from her cunt onto Eudoxia, slicking her thigh. Rocking forward, Eudoxia wiped her fingers through the evidence of Anna's arousal and stuck the juices inside herself.

The thought of mingling their fluids stoked her desire as she pushed deeper than ever before. She rode her fingers fast, and her orgasm teetered on the edge. She practically begged herself to come, but Xenia's moans stopped.

Eudoxia paused, her fingers slipping from between her folds.

Silence cloyed in the air until...

A tongue slipped inside her, and Eudoxia gasped. She reached for the hair and then ran her fingers through soft curls that were so often in a bun, hidden away. Eudoxia didn't have to look to know whose hair it was: Xenia.

Sucking her dry, Xenia moaned into her cunt, and the rumble vibrated Eudoxia's bones. She finally pulled up to look, and Anna was fucking Xenia with her mouth, her body tangled around Xenia's like a snake. Xenia trembled where she knelt, rocking her hips. Her breasts hung untouched.

This was Eudoxia's divine chance. It was like the gods smiled on her, allowing her to touch the afterlife. Eudoxia faced death with open arms.

Ignoring her oncoming orgasm, Eudoxia grabbed Xenia's breasts. They were...wonderful. Far more than what Eudoxia could've imagined or felt with her own.

Eudoxia brushed her fingers over Xenia's nipples as she had seen Anna do. They were hard, perked and pointed like they could cut diamonds. She massaged Xenia's breasts, touching the soft and the stiff. Perfection was a balancing act.

"More," commanded Xenia, and Anna's suckling sounds grew faster, louder. "More!"

Eudoxia realized Xenia was talking to her, so she kneaded her breasts. She pinched her nipples, twisting them in opposite directions, and it pushed Xenia over the edge.

Xenia screamed. Her whole body trembled. The feeling rushed up Eudoxia's arms, but she didn't slow her movements. The same way Anna didn't stop between Xenia's legs, fucking her until Xenia collapsed on the bed.

With Anna's help, Eudoxia had conquered the vampire queen. Xenia lay in a spent heap.

Anna climbed into bed too, pulling Eudoxia against her front. Anna's cool body was a breath of fresh air, and Eudoxia took in a lung full.

Anna nuzzled her neck. "I knew you'd be part of the family."

XII

While gray light leaked under the dark curtains, Eudoxia was slow to wake. She rolled in bed and rubbed her hand over the rumpled blankets, but she was alone like she always was in the morning.

Anna and Xenia would drink from her before the sun rose and then leave, hiding in the bowels of the house, and Eudoxia would sleep until she had regained her strength after a night of drinking, fucking, and loving. Sometimes, all three at once.

Based on her sore body and the light angling in straight down, it must've been noon. Her stomach grumbled. She ran a hand over her lower belly and then flopped to her side. She couldn't find the energy to peel herself out of bed yet.

The hearth crackled in the corner. Xenia must've put another log on before she left, just as she always did. Anna always wrapped a blanket around Eudoxia, tucking her into bed. Eudoxia loved it.

The nights were growing shorter, even if it was still cold outside. Winter was seeping away. Eudoxia had worked to make the house darker, buying thick dyed fabric and sewing it together to create curtains, but any sunlight would hurt Xenia and Anna.

Her stomach twisted, and her tongue turned to dust in her mouth. She rasped a breath. Was she dying?

After how many years she waited for death, she was now

happy, but her death still lingered in her peripheral vision.

Pushing off the bed, Eudoxia swayed. She needed to get to Anna and Xenia. Eudoxia didn't want to die!

Something dribbled down her thigh, and she swiped her hand across it. Goose bumps marred her skin. She didn't know what could be happening to her.

Bringing her hand into the light, she swallowed a small scream. She was bleeding.

The blood was different than when she cut her hand or when Anna and Xenia drank from her. It was congealed, filmy, brown globs stuck to her fingers.

When she turned back to the bed, the blood was red but thin and spotty, not what covered her fingers. It was a gush like a wound as if she had cut herself in the night. Even as she stood, the blood only slid from her one drop at a time.

Grabbing another cloth, Eudoxia wiped her slit and examined it further. It had been years since she last bled like this—when she had been a child and the madam thought she was a woman enough to do more at the whorehouse. Eudoxia had been trying to hide her menstruation from the madam, but it was eventually revealed. When Eudoxia left the whorehouse, she lost her meals and warmth, and her monthly cycles dried up. That changed living with vampires.

Eudoxia stood in shock, staring at the blood. What was she supposed to do? She barely remembered.

After cleaning herself up, she folded up clean rags and packed them between her legs, then she lined her underpants with more cloth.

She still reeked like blood, and while the scent normally didn't bother her, it smelled offensive now. She tried to wash, but the stench clung to her skin. It breathed from her cunt like a hot-blooded dragon.

No food smelled good, so she avoided the kitchen as well as anywhere else food might be. The whole house had a strong scent of mold and ash.

All that time cleaning had been wasted. She couldn't air out the house until nighttime. She had to get out.

In the end, she stood in the frozen courtyard behind the house. Snow covered the ground, and gray clouds hung overhead. She was still hot, her blood spilling from her. Wanting it to stop, she sunk into the snow and pressed her thighs together.

What would Anna and Xenia think? Everything had been happy, and Eudoxia was liking her life. She fucked it up.

Picking herself from the snow, she walked the length of the city but returned to the canal. It was just as it should've been because the canal was a vein of blood that breathed life. Now, the canal was covered in ice.

Eudoxia stopped at the edge, just as she had always done. If she fell, would she break through? Beneath the sheet of ice, her body would be pulled out to the harbor with each tug of the tide.

People ice skated, laughed, and children squealed in delight as they kicked a ball or played in the snow. Even in the long winters, everyone radiated joy.

Eudoxia stayed on the edge as the people dissipated, and darkness leaked in. She eyed any object she could throw into the canal and break the crust. The water would splash up and perhaps take her.

A hand landed on her shoulder, and Eudoxia jumped. Xenia stood beside her.

Darkness hooded her eyes, and she was as still as the crystalized canal. Her hand was just as heavy as the ice, pushing Eudoxia to stay where she was.

Eudoxia swallowed. "How did you find me?"

"We followed your scent," said Xenia.

Anna stepped to Eudoxia's other side. "And you smell delicious."

"I reek," said Eudoxia.

She was a slab of old meat.

Leaning toward Eudoxia, Anna sniffed her and then

moaned. "No."

She kissed Eudoxia's neck. Outside the house. Near taverns. Anyone could see.

Xenia watched the surroundings. If someone did see, Xenia would go on the hunt. Her own nostrils flared like she'd caught the scent.

Eudoxia moaned too. Her core tightened. The pain lessened, replaced by a wanting, but she felt the blood oozing from her.

"Let's go back to the house," said Anna, brushing Eudoxia's hair from her face. "I know what you'll like."

"Anna knows what *she* likes," muttered Xenia.

Anna laughed. "Eudoxia, you will yet be delicious. As will your cunt."

At the house, Xenia laid Eudoxia down on the bed as Anna kissed her neck. The throbbing between Eudoxia's legs increased. The pleasure pushed away the aching in her stomach and her lower back. Xenia threw off Eudoxia's clothes and massaged her tender breasts.

Her breasts weren't as wonderful as Xenia's, but they were sensitive now. Her nipples were the worst. Being outside had made them perked and hard. They hurt. So much of Eudoxia's body ached.

Xenia palmed her breasts, but her hands were cold. Frozen. The same with Anna, who kissed her. Eudoxia couldn't help the shiver running down her spine.

"I'll put more logs on the fire." Xenia peeled away.

Eudoxia wasn't able to catch her before she disappeared toward the hearth in the corner. Most of it was embers anyway.

"Let me warm you up." Anna trailed kisses down Eudoxia.

She nipped at Eudoxia's nipple, and Eudoxia now shuddered for a different reason. When Xenia returned, she took Eudoxia's other nipple.

Eudoxia fell back on the bed, and the two vampires followed her, sucking and licking. Pleasure rushed through her system, and she warmed. It crawled across her skin, starting with her chest and spreading to her appendages. She was splayed out on the bed, her limbs reaching for the four corners. She tried to reach further, expanding her body to give the two of them a touch.

"Xenia, do you have her nipples?" asked Anna with a devilish smirk.

"You know I do," said Xenia. "Save me some of the feast."

Laughing loudly, Anna dipped her head between Eudoxia's thighs.

Xenia licked one of Eudoxia's nipples and massaged her other breast. The pleasure only increased as Anna dragged her tongue up Eudoxia's slit.

Writhing on the bed, Eudoxia moaned. Each time she fucked Anna and Xenia, the pleasure only became better. She was very sensitive now—not just to the scent or to the pain —but how her body reacted to being touched. Something so small could set her alight.

"You taste wonderful," said Anna.

Eudoxia shook her head. "I don't understand how you can like it."

"It's you." Anna raised her head from between Eudoxia's thighs.

Blood smudged her lips and nose, a splash across her high forehead.

"It's your blood," continued Anna. "Your juices. Your cunt. Delicious."

Anna bowed her head into Eudoxia's slit again, and not a tick passed before the long strokes restarted. The pleasure was intense, only increasing with how Xenia sucked and massaged Eudoxia's breasts. Anna moaned as she drank, and it felt euphoric.

"Drink from me, Xenia," said Eudoxia breathlessly.

Xenia raised her head, silently questioning, and Eudoxia immediately regretted it. The pleasure slowed.

Eudoxia had said something she shouldn't have. The words

had flown from her lips before she thought about it, and they were out in the world, creating a rift between them. Eudoxia wanted to suck the words back inside, hiding them away like an animal did fruits and nuts before hibernation.

Then Xenia peeled back her lips, revealing her pointed fangs. It was partly a smile, completely a challenge. She looked so much like Anna in that moment. Xenia sunk her teeth into Eudoxia's breast and began to drink.

"Oh my...." Eudoxia gasped.

No other words did it justice. It was useless to try.

The pleasure compounded. Their tongues against Eudoxia's body and how they sucked. She trembled with lust and ache that turned to need.

Anna and Xenia gave into that need, feeding it, and Eudoxia screamed. She was caught in the undertow of the orgasm that she rode out the endless storm. She thrashed and fought. The hearth firelight flickered in her vision, and she couldn't breathe.

Now, she was ready for the afterlife.

Slowly, she regained her breath and her mind. The world returned to normal.

Anna pulled back her head, a large grin crossing her face, and Xenia licked the blood off Eudoxia's breast.

Anna and Xenia shared a kiss over Eudoxia.

XIII

One night, a month or so later, Eudoxia finished off a bottle of wine. Her mind swam. Her heavy head collapsed on Xenia's heavenly breast. A spirit sang in Eudoxia's head as a diabolical hunger coiled in her lower belly.

Eudoxia wasn't doing as much mending as she used to, instead spending her time sleeping or naked in the arms of her lovers. What a life this had become. It was foreign to what she thought she would be when she was a child.

Eudoxia tugged on Xenia's exposed breast, and Xenia set her in the chair. Wine didn't affect either of the vampires in the same way it did Eudoxia. Unlike them, she stumbled over her feet, and the world always swayed. Eudoxia should've stopped drinking the wine, but it tasted better than any she had ever had before. She could never returned to the stale ale of the pubs.

"Dance with me, Xenia!" Anna ripped Xenia away from Eudoxia.

The two women wrapped their arms around each other and began to dance. There was no music besides what Anna hummed, and after a moment, Xenia added a layer of harmonization. They moved in flashes and laughed, so happy.

Eudoxia leaned back on the bed, her stomach souring from the wine. Anna and Xenia had drank more but never slowed. They were impossible and brilliant. They were graceful even when funny. They were marvelous, put in the simplest terms.

Their lips touched, and their hands crawled over one another. Eudoxia only needed one guess to know where this would go next. Perhaps because of the wine or the love, the next words burst from her lips like she had never asked for anything before.

"I want to be like you," said Eudoxia.

The two vampires froze.

They could've been statues at the duke's castle. Visitors would gawk at their likeness to women, their skin like untouched snow, the beauty that took one's breath away.

It was definitely the wine in her system, decided Eudoxia, because she continued to swing her legs off the bed like a giddy child. She hadn't been a happy girl, yet here she was, floating like clouds. Now that she said the words, nothing felt better. The weight had been removed from her chest. She wanted to be alive. Well, dead...but undead.

"A vampire?" asked Xenia, like she was clarifying what Eudoxia wanted.

She asked it like no one would want to be a vampire, to have superior strength and speed, to love for eternity.

"Of course, she wants to be like us." Anna skipped to Eudoxia's side and slid an arm around her. "You want to be with us too?"

"Yes." Eudoxia nodded eagerly.

Her neck cracked, but the wine numbed any ache.

She continued in a rush, "I don't know how to explain it better, but I love you two. I've never been so happy. I've never wanted to live so much and so long."

Neither Anna nor Xenia replied.

Swelling tears—worried, emotional tears spilled down Eudoxia's cheeks. "I think about you day and night. I have never laughed more than when I am with you. You have completed me, and I want to spend eternity with you two. Do you want the same?"

"Of course, I do." Anna planted a kiss on her cheek.

Xenia said nothing, her lips thinned together. It was like when Eudoxia had first entered the house.

"Xenia?" prompted Eudoxia.

Her heart thundering wildly, and fear made her tremble, pushing the high of the wine from her body. She was sure she was about to be sick.

"Do you not want me?" asked Eudoxia.

"I do want you," said Xenia, voice soft. "However, to be a vampire...?"

Eudoxia didn't understand and turned to Anna as the middle person to explain. Anna patted her head like Eudoxia was a small child. The gesture did comfort Eudoxia, but her stomach was in knots. Perhaps she hadn't calculated the risk. Now, she very much blamed the wine.

"It's hard, Eudoxia," said Anna, "and Xenia doesn't like being a vampire."

Xenia scoffed forcibly, like a gust of wind blew through the bedroom. It fluttered Eudoxia's hair. She waited back.

"That's an understatement. You'll be giving up more than life, Eudoxia. More than breathing or the sun or food," listed Xenia, her voice losing its patient tone. "It's something that I still cannot explain after years of being a vampire."

"Yet we love our lives," said Anna, eyeing Xenia hard— another silent message that Eudoxia couldn't decipher.

After a pregnant moment, Xenia nodded curtly. Only once. It was all she was willing to budge.

Anna tightened her hold on Eudoxia's shoulders. "I'll turn you to one of us. If you so accept."

"I do," said Eudoxia eagerly, tilting her head and showing off her neck.

She was ready now.

Though she hadn't voiced these thoughts before, they had been rattling in her skull for some time, screaming to be let out. She had never opened her mouth, and now, she tried not to regret the situation.

"Not yet," said Xenia, and Eudoxia stilled. "First, you have to make a vow."

"Yes, you must." Anna slipped away and joined Xenia's side.

The swinging of Eudoxia's legs finally stopped, and she blinked at the two of them. Again, she didn't understand. Again, she was the outsider. It was almost enough to scare Eudoxia away.

Instead, Eudoxia presented herself. The vampires could have anyone they wanted, but they would choose her if Eudoxia did whatever they liked. She had already.

"What is the vow?" asked Eudoxia.

"We are married," said Xenia.

"Well, I'm married to a queen," said Anna, inclining her head to Xenia, but Xenia didn't move, ignoring Anna here. "We make a vow to each other because you won't just be a vampire, Eudoxia. You'll be our wife. We will be together for all eternity. We are a family, more than just vampires. Do you understand?"

She nodded, her head heavy but sharp. Blood pumped past her ears and freed the wine from her mind. Honestly, she was thinking clearly. Clearer than she had ever thought before.

The want stood before her, and hope spurred her forward.

"Say it aloud, Eudoxia," said Xenia. "Tell me you understand."

"I understand," said Eudoxia, "and I will become your wife."

XIV

A few nights later, Eudoxia dressed alone in her bedroom, waiting for night to descend over the house. She had barely slept through the day, anticipation and fear warring in her body. It was normal for women to be nervous on their wedding day, she thought.

However, she wasn't marrying a random man with a little coin to his name or a whore with no other prospects. She was marrying for love. It seemed impossible throughout her life, but her life had changed the moment she met Anna.

Anna and Xenia had let Eudoxia have the first choice of dresses tonight, and she had been diligent with the dress she chose, including the delicate stitching and the rich fabrics. Eudoxia had never cared before—not when she was a whore, knowing she'd shed those clothes quickly, and not when she was a woman without money and just trying to live.

But now, she dressed for Anna and Xenia. It was a role she would also play when she repaired their dresses and then made new ones. The designs swirled in her mind.

Eudoxia took care to wash and dress herself but stopped before putting on any paint. It wouldn't hide that she wasn't gorgeous or how her skin sagged and bones bulged from her flesh. Anna and Xenia loved her anyway.

The sun set into the shadows of night, and Eudoxia looked at herself in the mirror for the last time as a mortal. Once she was a vampire, she would've been memories.

She had asked what their lives had been like before, and Anna and Xenia had recited what they remembered. It wasn't much. They said Eudoxia's old life would slip away; Eudoxia didn't want it anyway. She was willing to strip it from her mind.

Her heart jumped to the base of her throat as she waited in the front room. Her cream-colored silk dress was soft against her skin. She swiped her hand up and down the sleeve stitched with snowflakes.

The hearth crackled, heat rushing through her body. It pooled in her hungry cunt, joining with love.

"You're gorgeous," said Xenia.

Eudoxia spun around, gasping. Her mind had been too focused on unimportant things.

She hadn't heard Xenia, but then again, Xenia was always silent, moving quieter than a mouse. Quieter than Anna too. It was how she effortlessly traveled through the shadows.

Xenia leaned against the doorway, wearing a dark dress. Her hair was piled high on her head, making her taller.

Eudoxia gulped. "You're stunning."

Xenia laughed. "I'm really not."

"You are."

"Nothing like you."

Eudoxia's cheeks warmed. "Shall I call you 'queen' tonight?"

Xenia rolled her eyes. "It's unnecessary."

"You never speak about it," said Eudoxia.

"Anna speaks about it enough," said Xenia, walking toward the hearth and Eudoxia.

"Where is she?"

"Still getting ready in the cellar. She loves a wedding, and her own was lackluster."

"What was it like?"

"Nothing like this. Nothing official," said Xenia. She ran her thumb over the sleeve of Eudoxia's dress. "It was more just us declaring our love for one another. We chose one another."

"Was this when you were a queen?" asked Eudoxia, half jesting.

Xenia gave a sad smirk. "You're not going to let that go, are you?"

"It's rare to meet a queen."

"Not as rare as you think."

"Anna said it was your husband—the king—who was a vampire."

Eudoxia had to ask before they wed. Xenia had never spoken about it, but Anna talked enough for the both of them. Eudoxia collected every piece of information like a scrap of food.

"He created you to be a vampire?" asked Eudoxia.

"I created myself," Xenia said, raising her chin.

"How is that possible?" asked Eudoxia.

Xenia stiffened, her lips thinned, and Eudoxia was scared she had pushed her too far. Wearing this dress and taking this vow might be for naught.

After a moment, Xenia said, "There was a woman, Kalina. My first love. My first wife. Neither of us were vampires, but we were married to the king, though not in so many words. He drank our blood and fucked us endlessly. We had no choice but to be his wives, and when he was bored of us, he threw us away."

Eudoxia's bottom lip trembled. The pain in Xenia's voice echoed in her chest. She tried not to rub at it.

"What happened to Kalina?" she asked in a small voice, never hearing of this woman before.

"She's dead." Xenia frowned. "She was caught stealing from our husband and giving back to the village."

"I'm sorry."

Her face was like stone, worn after years of erosion. "I swore I wouldn't allow that to happen to anyone else."

"So you became a vampire?"

"I did what I needed to do."

"And Anna?"

A smile tugged on Xenia's lips. "She was a light after a very long, dark year. She was a breath of life when I was dying. She was happiness and love. She made me realize I wasn't a monster."

"You've never been a monster, my queen." Anna stepped into the room, grinning.

The white satin and lace dress spilled around Anna. Her pale, bare toes peeked out. Paint highlighted her chiseled features, rounding her cheeks and enlarging her eyes. She was the embodiment of divine perfection.

Anna planted a kiss on Xenia's cheek and then turned. "You're stunning, Eudoxia."

She shook her head, flames eating up her arms. "I'm nothing compared to you."

"You must love yourself, Eudoxia," said Anna, "but we will love you more in return until you do."

"I love you both," said Eudoxia.

"We know." Anna kissed her on the cheek, her lips lingering.

Eudoxia waited for the kiss. The bite. The pleasure. She took a deep whiff.

Xenia touched Anna's shoulder and drew her back. "Wait until the wedding night, won't you?"

"It is hard." Anna flashed Xenia a smile. "It's a good thing you and I are already married."

She leaned in, but Xenia slipped away. Anna pouted at Xenia's back, and Eudoxia giggled. The familiarity was overpowering, the process repeating until the end of time. Eudoxia could imagine her wedding night and wedded life even a hundred years from now. Eternity laid out before her.

"Let us start tonight." Xenia extended her hand. "Eudoxia, will you join us?"

"Yes." Suddenly breathless, she tried to find her thoughts. Thankfully, her wedding dress hid her knocking knees.

Eudoxia took Xenia's outstretched hand, and Xenia took Anna. She led them into another room, one that Eudoxia had been warned from during the previous night and day. When she entered, she understood why.

She had walked into her own wedding as if she was a duchess, minus the priest and the cathedral. Flowers in vases sat around the room. Candles were lit haphazardly close to the curtains and sprawling fabric, more material than even the seamstress shop had. It explained why Xenia had put the wedding off for a few days and was distant. Eudoxia thought Xenia had been trying to talk Anna out of this marriage and they would run away together, leaving Eudoxia alone. Just as she had always been.

"This is...wonderful!" cried Anna.

Xenia brushed her knuckles over Anna's cheek, not that Anna actually cried. She placed her hands over her chest. Candlelight reflected in her moon-sized eyes. Eudoxia felt the same.

This was impossible for her wedding.

Anna never had a proper wedding, and while Xenia looked to not have cared, Anna was caught in the romance. Eudoxia wanted to be swept away too, but something gnawed in her bones.

She didn't deserve this.

This wasn't meant for her.

She didn't belong here.

Anna took Eudoxia's hand. "This is all for us. We are getting married. You shouldn't have done all this work by yourself, Xenia."

"Only the best for my wives." Xenia beamed before wincing. "I tried to hire musicians, but they started to ask too many questions. Then I had to..."

"It's the thought that counts," said Anna, "and I know you

gave many thoughts to this. Eudoxia, do you like it?"

She nodded, her voice caught in her throat.

No words could truly explain how she felt. How she floated. How happy, how scared. Though, she was sure her future wives heard her thundering heartbeat and smelled the sweat. Her dress clung to her skin, and she couldn't wait to strip it away. She questioned why she had chosen something so thick.

Xenia stepped toward the middle of the room, where the candles and flowers had been laid out. Eudoxia knew that it must've cost a fortune for all the flowers—for *any* flowers in winter—but the vampires could afford it.

Anna was getting the wedding she'd always wanted. Eudoxia would've been happy with something simple. However, when marrying a queen, pageantry was expected.

The three of them connected their hands, and together, they joined each other in matrimony. They gave each other blood and wrapped each other in fabric, tying each other together. Eudoxia was part of *her* family.

Their lips met before Eudoxia even had a chance to breathe, but breathing was mundane. Xenia and Anna never needed to break their kisses to breathe.

Eudoxia sucked in a deep breath and plunged into the kisses again. Hands traveled down her body. She wanted the dress to come away. She was on fire.

They had moved out of the wedding room and to one of the large bedrooms. Eudoxia hadn't wanted to move from the wedding, but the same couldn't be said for the vampires. Xenia had carried her up the stairs, depositing her on the floor.

"Take off my dress," whined Eudoxia, unable to hold Anna and remove her corset at the same time.

"You look so lovely," said Anna into her mouth. "Why ruin perfection?"

"I'm not perfection," said Eudoxia.

"You are," added Xenia, but she had already discarded a layer of clothing. She kicked off her skirt too, revealing her legs. Her breasts toppled over her corset.

Marveling at the milky clouds, Eudoxia began, "I'll only be perfection when—"

"Love yourself now," interrupted Anna in a hard purr. "You'll love yourself better when you are like us."

"Or you'll hate yourself," said Xenia.

"Isn't my love for you two enough?" asked Eudoxia.

She hadn't liked herself, her body, or anything of her soul in mortal form, so transforming into a vampire would've been her opportunity to be someone new. Someone better than her current self.

"For now, it's enough," said Anna.

"We'll work hard to convince you." Xenia stripped Eudoxia slowly, almost painfully.

Xenia took her time, and it was something Eudoxia needed to grow used to when becoming a vampire. She would have all the time she ever wanted.

She would move in a flash of an eye. She wouldn't age.

These were Eudoxia's last moments as a mortal, and she wanted them gone. However, she listened to what Xenia had said about being human. Eudoxia doubted she would miss it, but Xenia was wise beyond mortal years.

Anna took Eudoxia's mouth in her own, and Eudoxia fell into her. The opposite of Xenia was Anna, a light in the gloomy darkness. She was starlight and fresh air and the first day after winter. Anna traveled her lips over Eudoxia and then sucked on her neck. Anna never sunk in her teeth, but Eudoxia was ready.

As Anna kissed, Xenia tightened her grip on Eudoxia and took another layer of clothing off.

"Yours too, Anna," cooed Xenia.

"I thought you would never ask." Anna turned her back, swiping her hair from her neck. "Eudoxia, will you do the honors?"

There was nothing she wanted more.

With shaking hands, Eudoxia managed to undo the strings

on Anna's dress. The fabric pooled around her ankles. Anna was far more dressed than the rest of them, like a true bride and queen, but it was terrible to free her. Eudoxia peeled back the fabric as Xenia kissed her neck and down her shoulder blades, her bare body pressed against Eudoxia.

When Anna's clothes finally fell away, Eudoxia inhaled deeply. Her mind turned fuzzy, sight covered in a haze. Eudoxia had seen Anna and Xenia without clothes, but each time, she marveled. Her wedding night was no different.

Anna turned to Eudoxia, her mouth aimed toward her, as Xenia crept in behind. The two vampires locked their arms around her and ground their bodies against her.

She whimpered. Her cunt dripped.

Leaning around Eudoxia, Xenia kissed Anna. She giggled and wound her fingers through Xenia's hair. Xenia's breasts pushed into Eudoxia's back, and Eudoxia reached for them. The plushness was almost too much to bear. How dare her body not be able to contort, not allowing her to stretch.

At the same time, Xenia arched her back, jutting her hips forward, and dragged the lower part of her stomach against Eudoxia's lower back. Eudoxia's knees trembled, body vibrating. She thought she might fall.

Anna drove her hand down Eudoxia's torso, cupping her mound, and started to massage Eudoxia's nub.

Eudoxia moaned, and Xenia snaked her hand in as Anna made room. They had her whole slit, running up and down, flicking her bud. The pleasure became too much. Eudoxia couldn't remain standing any longer.

Xenia gathered her in her arms and laid her across the bed. Anna hopped in too. This was theirs, claimed by the number of times Eudoxia had come in it. Her blood and juices had leaked across the sheets.

Eudoxia reached for Anna's cunt, and Anna opened her thighs, letting out a soft moan. Her pointed teeth glistened in the firelight. Eudoxia rolled to her knees and pushed her fingers into Anna.

Suddenly, lips were upon Eudoxia's cunt, and she startled. The cool sensation cut the burning warmth yawning from her. Xenia ate her out. Her tongue and lips slid down Eudoxia's slit, and then her teeth grazed Eudoxia's bud.

Eudoxia lolled to the side, catching herself before she fell, but her hand had slowed. Anna grabbed Eudoxia and shoved her fingers up, moving her hand. Eudoxia became a doll. She allowed her limbs to be twisted for her loves' doings.

Xenia nipped at Eudoxia. Perhaps she meant to draw blood. It wouldn't be the first time.

Anna roared in orgasm, which pushed Eudoxia closer to the edge. Xenia was already sucking on her pearl. Pleasure curled around Eudoxia's neck, threatening to strangle her. Xenia worked so hard for her own wedding and wedding night. Eudoxia wanted Xenia to come with them. Now.

Thankfully, Anna grabbed Xenia's cunt and started to stroke it. Xenia was quick to mewl. Anna played Xenia's body expertly. Xenia fell forward, orgasming straight into Eudoxia. It made Eudoxia come.

Breathing hard, Eudoxia fell onto the bed. Life flashed before her eyes, the hearth dimming and blazing. Her body buzzed. She had lost control of her limbs.

Anna kissed Eudoxia's belly, and Xenia brushed back Anna's hair and said, "She's tired, Anna. Let her breathe."

"She'll be ready to go again soon. Won't you, Eudoxia?" asked Anna. Firelight twinkled her eyes.

Eudoxia nodded, unable to talk or breathe. Her heart felt like it would explode from her chest. Her blood would paint the walls, the bed, and her wives. Her loves would lick her blood, cleaning her corpse with their tongues. Their long strokes would find her in the afterlife.

"Give me a moment," said Eudoxia when she finally found her breath.

"How about you rest?" asked Xenia, patting the inside of Eudoxia's thigh. Her forefinger touched the vein that she had drunk from so often.

"No," said Eudoxia. She didn't need to rest, not when she was married to vampires.

Anna knocked her shoulder against Xenia's leg. "See?"

Xenia shook her head. She was trying to send a silent message to Anna, but the other vampire ignored it.

Anna trailed kisses up Eudoxia's leg, raising Eudoxia from near death again.

XV

T he wedding night had been wonderful, but Eudoxia hated that morning was on the horizon.

Eudoxia had the rest of her life with them, but how did she explain all that happened in the past night? How alive it made her feel. Without Anna and Xenia at her side, she was sure she would've died.

Their limbs intertwined, and Anna laid her head upon Eudoxia's chest, smiling probably because of her quickened heartbeat. It hadn't relaxed since they started to kiss.

"When will you two return to the cellar?" asked Eudoxia, tightening her hold on Anna.

She didn't want to let go, even though the vampire could've slipped from her grasp like water. Same with Xenia.

Eudoxia didn't want to be in this bed alone. She would've gone back to her old bedroom with a small bed, where she always slept alone. It felt better in a smaller bed. She had once tried to sleep here but had felt too lonely. She had tossed, reaching for her loves that weren't there.

"You'll be joining us in the cellar after..." Anna gripped Eudoxia's wrist, her fingertips pressing into her vein.

Confusion coursing through her, Eudoxia widened her eyes. "What do you mean?"

"You said you wanted to be like us. Is that still true?" asked Xenia, hesitant.

It was the same hesitancy from when she questioned Eudoxia about this vampiric life. Eudoxia had thought Xenia was finally accepting her, so what had changed?

Xenia brushed her finger up Eudoxia's thigh.

"I do want to be like you," said Eudoxia breathlessly. "I am your wife. I want to spend the rest of my life with you."

Anna beamed, and Xenia smirked.

"Only clarifying." Something patiently sad resounded in Xenia's voice as she climbed from the bed and gathered a robe.

Eudoxia bit back a whine. Xenia's covering herself was doing Anna and Eudoxia an injustice.

Rolling her eyes, Anna sat up. "Don't listen to her, Eudoxia. Xenia grows on you, but there's a reason she's kept us safe for so long. This is dangerous."

"I know," said Eudoxia.

It was more than being a dangerous vampire. It was about them as a family: three women living together and in love. There were many who wouldn't understand and even more who would tear them apart.

Eudoxia only wanted to be happy. She had waited so long and wouldn't let go of this newly built treasure.

Anna flicked her eyes to Xenia, whose lips were pursed in thought. Then, with one nod, the conversation ended as quickly as it began.

Anna crept forward in the bed.

Eudoxia raised her head, heart rattling in her rib cage. Was it time?

"Are you ready?" asked Anna.

Eudoxia gulped. "Do you mean now? Here?"

She'd thought they would do it in the cellar.

"Yes," said Xenia, coming to the edge of the bed in a flash. "Anna will be changing you."

Anna nodded, her fangs peeking through her thin pale lips. She wore a coy smile, but her eyes gave away her true intentions.

Even though Eudoxia would soon be able to move as fast as her wives, it scared where when she looked straight into Anna's soul.

"Not you, Xenia?" asked Eudoxia.

Anna pouted.

Taking her hand, Eudoxia added, "Not that I'm not happy it's you."

"I know." Anna laughed. "Xenia will keep an eye out. Like she said, *danger*. She'll get you your first meal. You'll want to drink it quickly. It'll help you change."

Eudoxia knew all of this. Xenia had walked through every step—multiple times—like it would change Eudoxia's mind.

"So...." Anna trailed her fingers across Eudoxia's wrist. "Are you ready?"

She raised her limb as a gift. "Yes."

"She'll be drinking from your neck." Xenia inclined her head.

Her hair tumbled in the way, waves washing down her back. Using a leather cord, Xenia drew her hair into a bun at the base of her skull.

Anna and Xenia had drunk from Eudoxia's neck before, especially after they had begun to fuck. Xenia had been skittish, but Eudoxia's pleasure was better when they sank their teeth into her neck, halfway between her head and heart.

Eudoxia couldn't wait to drink blood like she had seen Anna do to Xenia. It was erotic. Tender. Pleasurable. It had haunted Eudoxia's dreams, made her come while she slept.

Anna lingered over Eudoxia's wrist and then touched her shoulder. "Relax on the bed."

Eudoxia squirmed and closed her eyes, taking deep breaths. Relaxation seemed so far away, but it soon washed over her like a cool wave. She trusted her two wives.

Suddenly, Xenia said, "There will be no going back."

"Xenia!" Anna gasped. "Don't—"

"It's the truth. There is no way to stop the process," said Xenia.

Her cold hand took Eudoxia's.

"Once we start—truly start…" She paused and lowered her chin. "You'll be one of us. A vampire. It will be painful."

"I know." Eudoxia squeezed Xenia's hand, peeking through her eyelashes at her wife's concerned face. "All will be well."

Eudoxia was scared—she couldn't hide it—but the pressure released from her chest because she was taking this jump with the others. It reassured her that they were as frightened as her.

"I love you, Eudoxia," said Xenia.

Eudoxia smiled. "I love you too, Xenia, and you, Anna."

"I love you both." Anna curled her arms around the two, holding them close, and then she pushed Eudoxia back against the bed. "Now, shall we get on with this? We will want her change starting before morning. Xenia, when will you hunt?"

"Once she drinks your blood," said Xenia, then laid a hand on Anna. "We could wait until tonight to transform her because the oncoming morning. We'll have more time—"

"Now," ordered Eudoxia, cutting Xenia off.

Anna raised her eyebrows, also challenging Xenia.

The vampire queen would do her best to wiggle out of this, holding Eudoxia at bay for another year—if not more. Eudoxia knew her wife only wanted them safe, but she never felt so as a mortal. Perhaps it came back to how many times she had wished for death, morphing it in her head like an artist twisted clay. Another day in her mortal form was another day that she missed out on eternity with her loves.

Xenia glanced between them, drawing her eyebrows together. Her lips curved into a frown.

"Please," Eudoxia practically begged, "now. Let us start our lives together fully."

She couldn't wait any longer.

Xenia still held Eudoxia's hand but knelt on at bedside. Eudoxia was safe in her hands, and she was safe as Anna neared, her fangs extended.

Eudoxia had long accepted that she would die but hadn't considered she would meet two loves, let alone that they would be two powerful women. It never would've been possible if Eudoxia had thrown herself in the canal.

Anna licked the length of Eudoxia's neck.

Anticipation slithered through her, and she curled her other hand into the blankets, holding herself back before she grabbed Anna and brought her lips down. If she acted on those urges, they would fuck again, and Eudoxia would have to wait another day to be a vampire. To make love as a vampire.

Anna sucked on Eudoxia's neck over her pulse. Eudoxia moaned, her back arching. Her body craved another release, and Eudoxia would need the gods' strength to keep herself composed.

After less than a moment, Anna sunk her teeth into Eudoxia.

She let out a small scream.

The pain was different—more than her blood being drunk. She writhed on the bed. It felt like poison burning through her veins.

Steel-like hands locked over her legs and torso, and Eudoxia tried to fight them off. It had to be Xenia. Who else?

Was it always this painful?

Eudoxia's throat grew raw from screaming.

Scorching blood pooled under her body. It coated her skin. She couldn't do this. Didn't *want* this.

She punched Anna, but her fist met cold stone. The same stone barred her body. She couldn't slide in the bed. It had lost the heavenly feeling.

Eudoxia was sinking into the afterlife, the darkness about to consume her. She had to claw her way out of this.

"Relax," cooed Xenia from somewhere distant. "Breathe, Eudoxia. Breathe through this."

"Stop," Eudoxia groaned through clenched teeth.

"Anna, hasten," said Xenia.

That order only made Anna pull harder, deeper, sucking Eudoxia until she was dry. With how much she drained, she must've taken Eudoxia's marrow, eating the organs like they were a delicacy.

While Eudoxia tried to fight Anna off, the vampire felt as heavy as a boulder in the canal.

Eudoxia was sinking, close to hitting the bottom of the abyss that never came.

Xenia said, "I'll leave to get Eudoxia her first meal. Give her your blood."

The tension released off Eudoxia's lower body.

A moment later, Anna's teeth withdrew, and Eudoxia sucked in shaky breaths.

Each breath burned. Her stomach wiggled like a parasite was embedded in her. Her bones were turning to steel, forged in heat and embers. She was sure she was going to vomit and turned her head.

Pain leeched from the side of her neck. She forced her eyes open to the carnage: her blood splayed across the bed. She didn't know how she could lose so much and be alive.

"Breathe, Eudoxia," called Anna. "You'll drink my blood now."

Eudoxia turned her head away from the vampire. She didn't want the blood.

"You'll feel better," said Anna.

Her wrist hung over the lower half of Eudoxia's face, blood bubbling out, skin torn.

"Eudoxia, drink," said Anna.

She would never.

"Drink, Eudoxia." Anna pressed her hand to Eudoxia's mouth, but her wound had already healed, no longer shedding blood.

"Shit," Anna hissed and ripped into her skin again, more

blood bubbling to the surface.

Anna grabbed Eudoxia's jaw and opened it, nearly breaking her jaw. Her fingers were like iron, nails digging into Eudoxia.

More pain crushed her body. Eudoxia screamed.

"I'm sorry," said Anna, "but you need to drink."

Blood dripped into Eudoxia's mouth, landing on her tongue. She gagged. It fell into the back of her throat and burned.

Where was the pleasure she'd been promised?

Where was the pleasure she once had?

The blood seeped into her, but it wasn't enough. Not after all Eudoxia had lost.

"Shit." Anna ripped open her wrist again.

More blood.

Not enough.

It caught in her throat.

"Swallow the blood," ordered Anna, slamming Eudoxia's jaw shut.

Eudoxia was sure she heard her teeth crack, but she couldn't feel it.

She couldn't feel a lot.

Perhaps her ragged breathing.

Her slowed heartbeats.

"Drink, Eudoxia!"

The words roared through her body, rattling her empty rib cage.

She was dissolving into the bed.

"Xenia, where are you?" Anna's words were louder, gurgled in the water. "Xenia, I need you. Xenia!"

She jumped off the bed and ran away.

Eudoxia couldn't chase her like she had tried before.

"Xenia, where are you?"

Gone to get Eudoxia her first meal as a vampire.

Vampire.

Eudoxia had forgotten what she was becoming. Why Anna took her blood and made her drink in return.

The simple need for survival flooded through her. She forced thoughts aside and gulped the blood down her throat. It settled deep in her gut. She sucked any remaining blood from her teeth and swallowed again.

Anna stomped back into the room. "Xenia's gone!"

Eudoxia gulped. "She was getting me someone to eat."

Anna halted. "You're speaking? And not screaming."

She flashed to the side of the bed, and Eudoxia grimaced. She wasn't used to that yet. How soon until she would move so fast?

Anna took her hand. "How are you?"

"Tired." Her tongue turned to dust, and her nose twitched.

What was that she smelled? Blood but something mustier. It reminded her of mold.

"You need to rest." said Anna in a soothing tone. "When you wake, Xenia will have returned with your first meal."

"I don't want to sleep." Eudoxia yawned.

Exhaustion gnawed at her bones like maggots worming into dead bodies. They burrowed in her organs and under her skin.

"You'll feel better," said Anna, brushing back Eudoxia's hair. It stuck to her forehead with sweat.

Eudoxia groaned, "No."

"Every vampire must do it. It helps with the process. You'll be a vampire when you wake."

A cold heaviness crawled over her. Lying on a bed, it felt like her body was seeping into the canal. Where was the bottom?

Eudoxia gasped and blinked her eyes open.

Anna hovered over her, worry creasing her beautiful face. Gray light leaked in from somewhere in the house, curling nearer. Anna couldn't be in the light. It would hurt her.

"You need to go," said Eudoxia, trying to push her away. Her hand tapped Anna before falling back to the side. Eudoxia was still powerless to move her wife, but...

One day, she thought.

Anna growled, "Xenia isn't back yet. Xenia!"

The sound hurt her ears, and Eudoxia flinched. "You would hear her."

"We need to move," snarled Anna, whipping her gaze between the door and the windows.

Eudoxia was comfortable here, not that she remembered where she was. Somewhere in a house, yes? Where had they bitten her?

Anna gathered Eudoxia in her arms, and Eudoxia's head lolled to the side. Her neck ached. Anna wasn't as plush as Xenia, but she was just as strong. And fast.

Gray light flashed before Eudoxia's eyes, and her body jerked as Anna jumped to avoid the small slivers of light. The sun slipped through the curtains, its rays creeping across the floor like spiders. Tendrils reached out to grab them. Then it went dark.

A door slammed behind her. Cold moisture overtook Eudoxia. She was laid on something hard.

"Are you all right?" asked Anna.

"Just tired." As Eudoxia said the words, a shiver ran down her body.

"I don't have any blankets or clothes. Why didn't we dress you?" Anger burned through Anna's words until she was screaming, the sound ricocheting off the cellar's stone walls.

"I didn't want to get blood on the dress." Eudoxia slurred.

Her words rushed around her head, her hearing ebbing. She wasn't sure she said the words aloud.

"We should've waited until tonight. Xenia was right, and now she is—you are—" Anna hung her head.

Eudoxia tried to reach for Anna, her arm wouldn't move from the hard surface. Her body was sinking like melting snow.

She wished she was back on the soft bed.

Yawning again, Eudoxia fought to keep her eyes open, but it was useless. She was surrounded in darkness. She hated the cellar, and she had only been here for a moment.

"Rest, Eudoxia," whispered Anna. "I'll wake you when Xenia returns. You'll feast then."

Eudoxia's tongue went slack, and her empty belly cawed for more food.

No. Not food or water.

Blood.

Without blood, she would wither. She needed to drink.

"Calm, Eudoxia." Anna's voice fluttered to her ears.

"Blood," croaked Eudoxia, her mouth like sand.

Her throat burned, hurting as much as it had when Anna had been drinking from her.

Infecting her.

"Xenia isn't back yet," said Anna. "It's only midday."

"Blood," repeated Eudoxia.

"Not yet."

Eudoxia reached for Anna, gripping her arm and digging in her nails. Saliva oozed from her mouth. The least Anna could do was give Eudoxia blood.

"Let go." Anna wrenched her arm away. "It's not my blood you need."

"Help me up," said Eudoxia, her breath coming out as a wheeze.

Did she even need to breathe? When would she stop breathing as a vampire?

"I'll find someone to drink." She tried to push up but faltered back on the wood table.

Pain coursed through her. Why was she in pain? She was supposed to be a vampire.

Immortal!

She was so weak. Worse than when she had been human.

"Rest, Eudoxia," said Anna. "You'll feel better after you rest —"

"Stop saying that," snarled Eudoxia, digging her nails into the wood. "I'll feel better after I drink."

She had more to say—she would never stop talking—but she worked her jaw, unsure where to start. Her wives had failed her. They were killing her!

"You still need to slumber." Anna touched her forehead to Eudoxia's.

It was the touch of her wife, and Eudoxia missed it. She loved that touch.

"I feel like I'm dying," cried Eudoxia, rolling on the table.

"You're not dying," said Anna, locking her arms on Eudoxia.

The petite woman, made of steel, pressed her down. Anna's weight felt heavier than the rush of the canal at high tide, stronger than the doors slammed in Eudoxia's face when she left the whorehouse. More powerful than any man who pushed Eudoxia around when she'd been a whore.

"I *am* dying," pleaded Eudoxia through gasps.

Eudoxia's body turned to lead. Her blood was sluggish. Her limbs were not her own.

"You'll be fine." Anna bit her bottom lip, and her fang cut her lip, drawing blood.

Eudoxia lurched up, chasing it, but Anna flew across the cellar. She knocked into the wall. Dusty glass wine bottles tumbled from the wooden shelves and shattered across the stone. Eudoxia jumped from the table, but her knees gave out. She crumbled.

Glass stuck into her skin, more pain layering on top of what already pushed through her. She screamed, and after a moment, those screams transformed into dry sobs.

She rolled in the glass, the shards stabbing her. She sucked in stale, moldy air. It crept into her lungs, and it hurt her from inside out. Each breath sent a jolt down her body, cracking her bones. Her blood boiled and slid out as she melted to slush on the floor.

"Eudoxia, can you hear me?" Anna stood back, her lip healed. "Eudoxia?"

She couldn't unlock her jaw.

Anna ventured a step closer, her fingernails like talons, her fangs peeking out. The best predator that ever existed: a vampire.

"Eudoxia, I'm going to pick you up and put you back on the table," said Anna.

Eudoxia tried to move her head, but she had turned to stone. The same stone that created Anna and Xenia's bodies, their skin hardened into steel.

There was no movement now without pain. Not even to blink.

Vampires didn't blink; Anna and Xenia never did. It was no more startling than their lack of breathing.

Eudoxia's rushed breaths rubbed against her throat. Her heartbeat had slowed but thundered in her ears. Her body was trying to survive.

"I'm going to pick you up." Anna snaked her arms under Eudoxia's body and lifted her from the floor.

It was a repeat of before, but instead of her body going limp, Eudoxia was a stick, her legs and arms splayed out, her head tilted at an awkward angle.

Anna set Eudoxia on the table and smoothed a hand over her forehead. Her touch sent Eudoxia screaming again.

"Oh, Eudoxia, what's happening to you?" Anna hovered over her, half of her face cast in shadows of gray light leaking through the ajar door at the top of the stairs.

Anna flinched—she couldn't be in the light—but she held Eudoxia's hand. The pressure of her grip shattered Eudoxia's bones, tearing apart her skin. Eudoxia was turning to glass when she was meant to be hardening.

"This wasn't supposed to happen," cried Anna. "This wasn't like me. Or Xenia. Xenia should be here. She'll know what to do."

Eudoxia didn't know what was happening.

"You're bleeding. Your wounds aren't healing. You're..." Anna backed up a step. "This shouldn't be happening! I think you're dying, Eudoxia."

This was how she imagined the most painful death. Nothing like the canal where she would sink deep inside and slowly disappear in the water, lost under the ice.

"No. No. No," repeated Anna. "No, no, no, no, no! NO!"

Her head slashed back and forth. Her hair swished through the air like a whistle.

Anna threw the shelves off the wall. The wood broke, and more glass shattered.

Eudoxia internally grimaced. Anna was too loud.

All of it was too loud. Even her thoughts.

Rumbling, crumbling sounds reached Eudoxia.

"Anna," Eudoxia tried to say. She tried to reach for her, but nothing moved. "Anna."

She came to Eudoxia. "I'm sorry. This is all my fault."

Eudoxia wanted to say no.

"You're dying because of me. I failed you," continued Anna. "I'm sorry. I should've let you continue with your life—in the tavern, in the seamstress shop, in the whorehouse. Xenia told me to do so, but I wanted you so bad. I saw you and really thought you needed me."

I did need you, Eudoxia tried to say.

Nothing.

Even that thought was fleeting.

Like her breath.

Like her heartbeat.

"I shouldn't have chosen you," said Anna, her voice wavering. "Something about you just drew me in. You looked so sad, and I understand—or I thought I understood. I've been lonely and sad too, even Xenia. We've been looking for another person to join our family for a long time. Eudoxia, can you forgive me?"

Yes. She tried to force the word past her sealed lips.

Her vision had darkened, more than the shadows hanging around the cellar. The gray light coming from the ajar door blinked out. She couldn't fight the haze covering her. It pushed down on her until her chest couldn't move.

How did she still breathe? Each rasp grazed the inside of her. So shallow.

Unlike the depths to which she was falling.

Water was lapping over her body, slipping over her limbs like claws and threatening to pull her under. It was cold. It slowed her heartbeat more.

Why was death so close yet held back? What did it wait for?

Eudoxia was splayed open, weakened.

Her sight and smell were gone. She thought she would taste nothing either. She couldn't swallow if Anna had shoved more blood inside of her. No blood would save her.

"Eudoxia?" asked Anna, her voice distant. "Can you hear me? I hear your heartbeat. Your breaths. Hold to life. Xenia will be here soon. You'll get blood."

No more, she wanted to beg.

"Xenia, quick!" Anna's voice pitched up an octave. "Eudoxia's dying!"

Those words were too simple for what Eudoxia felt.

"Drink," ordered Xenia, her voice near. "Drink the blood, Eudoxia. It's human. It will make you one of us."

Something brushed Eudoxia's lips. She still felt something, even if she couldn't move.

"Anna, open her jaw," commanded Xenia.

Something *popped*.

Something touched her.

All out of reach.

Drip. Drop. Drip.

The sound rushed down her body, disappearing into her sunken depths.

Plop.

"Eudoxia, drink the blood," ordered Xenia. "All you need to do is swallow."

"She's dying," cried Anna.

"No," growled Xenia.

"Something's wrong! We didn't do it right."

"We did it right."

"Then it was my blood. It poisoned her."

"That's not true, Anna."

"It has to be, Xenia. You didn't have this issue with me! She can't die."

"She can."

"We're vampires. We're supposed to be able to give life as much as we take it. We gave her life."

"No, we've taken her life away."

"Don't say that, Xenia!"

"It's true, Anna."

"I know I shouldn't have chosen Eudoxia. This is my fault."

"It isn't."

"Eudoxia, can you hear me?" asked one of those heavenly voices, quieted by the constant dripping. "Eudoxia, please stay —"

"Don't ask her that, Anna," said the second voice. "She cannot control it."

"She's dying!"

"I hear it."

"We need to—"

"Eudoxia, be free. Don't wait on us. Let your pain go."

"Xenia, don't—"

"It's what needs to be done, Anna."

"You're killing her."

"I'm helping her."

"It's still her death."

Kill or help? Life or death? The undead.

Vampires.

The water and chill finally overtook her. She was drowning. She tried to slash through the waves, but she couldn't escape.

No escape.

Fear. Pain.

Make it end, she begged as she sunk to the bottom of the canal.

"Xenia, don't!"

Snap.

Also by Sophia-Rose Johnson

The Castle of Skull Series
Castle of Skulls
Counts Her Souls
By She Who Is Death-Touched

Mermaids of Lake Superior Series
Beneath the Surface
Thaw the Heart

The Coven Thirteen Series
The Favorite Kind of Wild Magic
The Least Kind of Controlled Magic

The MacLeod Trilogy with Susan Stradiotto
Fight for Darkness
Hunger for Darkness
Conquer the Darkness
Poisoned Darkness with Susan Stradiotto

Stand-alone Novels
Temptation of a Haunted Heart

Short Stories
"Bloody Mary's Day Off" in *Twice Upon a Name*
"The Haunting of Neve Ravensblood" in *Third Name's a Charm*
"The Prophecy of a Powerful Witch" in *Four Names of Fortune*

Acknowledgments

Firstly, I would like to thank you, the reader, for taking the time to read this. Thank you!

Secondly, I would like to thank every person who helped me write and edit this book from the first draft to final edits. Thank you, Susan Stradiotto, for being my copy editor, mentor, and friend. I would like to give special thanks to my beta readers: Bailey Merlin, E.A. Spellman, and Taylor Harrison.

Thirdly, I would like to thank everyone else who would take up a whole book on their own. This book (and series) was like stepping into a new world and role for me, allowing me to experiment and experience new things. This series offered me a new opportunity, and I fell in love with it and every wife.

With each of the stories, I feel a connection to the main character, and Eudoxia was no different. Writing *The Thread She Unraveled* was cathartic, opening up the parts of myself that I keep locked away from the rest of the world. I've explored mental health in a number of my stories, but Eudoxia was the probably the one character that dove deep into what I feel like with depression. Unfortunately for her and others, there aren't always happy endings. I wish you the best in your journey.

Once again, thank you all who read this book and support me as an author.

- Sophie

About the Author

Sophia-Rose Johnson, who has also written under S. Johnson, is from Minnesota, USA, and is a northerner by heart and accent. She graduated from the University of Wisconsin-Superior in 2018 with a writing degree. While she first published in 2022, she's been writing since 2011. She is a queer woman.

Stay connected with her via social media or website: www.sjohnsonbooks.com/